A
CHARMED LIFE

Celebrating Wicca Every Day

By
Patricia J. Telesco

NEW PAGE BOOKS
A division of The Career Press, Inc.
Franklin Lakes, NJ

A CHARMED LIFE
Cover design by Cheryl Finbow
Printed in the U.S.A. by Book-mart Press

To order this title, please call toll-free 1-800-CAREER-1 (NJ and Canada:
201-848-0310) to order using VISA or MasterCard, or for further
information on books from Career Press.

The Career Press, Inc.
3 Tice Road, PO Box 687,
Franklin Lakes, NJ 07417
www.careerpress.com
www.newpagebooks.com

Library of Congress Cataloging-in-Publication Data

Telesco, Patricia, 1960-
    A charmed life : celebrating Wicca every day / by Patricia J. Telesco.
        p.   cm.
    Includes bibliographical references and index.
    ISBN 1-56414-487-9 (pbk.)
    1. Witchcraft. 2. Witches—Conduct of life. I. Title.

BF1566 .T33 2000
        133.4'3—dc21   00-035514

Dedication

This book honors my extended magickal family, especially those who have come into my life recently. To Otter, Sandy, Ambrose, Rose, and so many others who have extended the hand of unqualified friendship, I would like to say thank you. You keep me sane on those days that are anything but! Also to Arawn, Betsy, Rowan, Walker, Don, Danielle, Griffin, Corwyn, T'Sa, Kat, Wade, AJ, Sirona, Dorothy, Fritz, Wren, Diane and the "gang" from the gatherings who have become a safe haven in life's storms—I miss you when we are apart, and celebrate when we are together.

Memorial

In memory of Blythe, who graciously donated her body to science so that other women might not suffer the horrors of uterine cancer. Your gift, as your life, will not be forgotten. May your spirit fly free and may you find peace in the arms of the Sacred.

Contents

Introduction

The motivation for working magic is unlike superstition—it is not fear, it is the desire to understand.
—Marion Weinstein

Witches haven't always had a terrific reputation, to say the least. Even in today's New Age, remnants of this reputation linger in our awareness. It's impossible for Halloween to go by, for example, without the traditional, superstitious portrait of witches with warts, black hats, and wicked cackles. These decorations and sound effects are provided by unassuming celebrants who often don't realize that Wicca is a viable religion and spiritual path for thousands of people—people such as you and me who are striving to understand their place in the greater scheme of things—people who rediscover the spark of magick in their hearts and want to release that energy into every corner of life.

That's a tall order! And what makes it even more challenging is remaining aware of how 2,000 years of bad press has affected magickal traditions. Consider how others think about

Wicca, and how this affects your capacity to lead a truly spiritual life surrounded by those doubts and misrepresentations. For example, how many times do we shy away from a conversation about holiday celebrations at the office or put away our magickal books and tools when relatives come to the house? While I'm not an advocate of bellowing one's beliefs from the rooftops, I suspect I'm not alone in my frustrations about hiding my faith to protect myself from unjust treatment or for propriety's sake. It should not be so, and part of this book's goal is to help you find creative ways to overcome this difficulty.

Even outside society's structures there's the very real possibility that modern Witches, experienced or not, sometimes unwittingly fall into a different stereotype trap. Specifically: Do we don our jewelry and robes and enact our rites in ways that are really meaningful, or because we think that's what someone else expects? If you answered the latter, don't feel bad—you are certainly not alone. It's quite common for human beings to want approval from those whom we admire. However, if our Witchcraft is to be really transformational we must also find approval in our own minds and spirits.

A Charmed Life advocates an aware, informed, proactive way of weaving our magick so that spirituality is no longer secondary to the daily grind. It is designed in such a manner to positively and magickally rebuild our selves, our living spaces, and every corner of our workaday world without necessarily upsetting our already time-challenged schedules. In the pages of this book, you'll discover that an integrated magickal lifestyle can become a driving force for making your reality everything you wish it to be—metaphysically, mundanely, and much more!

A Charmed Life reminds each of us that magick is accessible to anyone, and a viable, meaningful means of taking control of today and tomorrow. You'll begin seeing magick as a wholly natural birthright that you can reach out and claim, here and now. No matter where we live, work, love, or play, everything in our daily routines can become an expression of metaphysical principles if we foster our spirits dutifully.

Along the same lines, this book will help you bring the power, beauty, music, and magick back into the word *Witch*, so that you can sing it loudly in the new millennium without fear and prejudice. By truly learning to "walk the walk" and make every part of your life a reflection of magickal ideals, you can help change the way Wiccans are received for all time to come. Better still, living in this manner will break down the walls that have separated our mundane selves from Spirit.

A Charmed Life is effectively a Book of Shadows, a bible of sorts, aimed at creating peace within, harmony without, and a knowingness that reaches beyond words. By applying the activities and hints in these pages—along with a little ingenuity—the modern Witch can use Earth-aware philosophies mingled with today's realities for formulating transformational, life-affirming magick, anytime, anywhere! Magick does not have to be the enemy of science or technology. Everything in this world holds potential for our Witchery if we use an imaginative eye that's willing to see beyond the surface and seize the possibilities!

Taking this tact keeps magick from becoming stale and mechanical, and it encourages us to let Wicca grow and change with our society, the Earth, and, most importantly, our hearts. By so doing we can start gathering the best from the past and present of our respective traditions, then look to the future with a hopeful, prepared eye.

Let's venture forward together, building a present and future filled with positive, evolutionary magick. Let's begin living a truly witchy life today!

Note: *A Charmed Life* was written for anyone interested in living a magickal lifestyle, whether you live in a city, suburb, or the country. Be that as it may, if you consider yourself a "beginner" who may not understand all the terms and methods used in this book, I highly recommend reading any of the following of my other books as adjuncts to your ongoing spiritual education:

♦ *Magick Made Easy*

♦ *Victorian Grimoire*

♦ *Spinning Spells, Weaving Wonders*

♦ *Shaman in the 9-5 World*

(Publication information for these books can be found in the Appendix.)

There are many other fine writers in the magickal community who can round out your vision of the diversity of the Craft, including Sirona Knight, Dorothy Morrison, and A.J. Drew.

Additionally, for information on Wicca, Paganism, gatherings, and all things magickal, go to ***www.witchvox.com***.

Patricia Telesco
July 2000

Chapter 1

Mind Over Mundanity

The proper study of mankind is man.
　　　　—*Alexander Pope,* Essay on Criticism

All magick begins with thought and will, but to really understand and apply it, we first have to better understand how the human mind works. In turn, the study of human thought and our enduring quest for "enlightenment" naturally leads to exploring culture, language, and the amazing human capacity for growth and change. Unfortunately, this exploration has been met with apathy, even among Witches. People wonder, "What difference does it all make?" The way people thought about and sought out spiritual truths in the past, and the way we do so today, makes a *big* difference in our world and our magick.

Fleeting doubts and insecurities undermine not only your magick, but everything you hope to achieve in this life. *A Charmed Life* will build self-esteem, not destroy. Step one, therefore, is to mentally take back the driver's seat in our attitudes. Step two is to become more intimately aware of our divine nature and to tap the wisdom, power, and truths that it represents.

Meditation is one way of doing both. Effective meditation reshapes our thought-forms and retrains our minds to far more positive ways of pondering, acting, and living. It opens the way inward and upward to a mental space where we can commune with ourselves or the God/dess. We must remain realistic regarding our goals here. No one learns how to meditate effectively overnight. But with time and practice you can begin to act in accord with magickal thought, which in turn sends out positive energy on all levels and builds a more harmonious, functional foundation for living a Wiccan lifestyle in today's hectic world.

Don't let the idea of meditation scare you off. You already meditate on some level every day just by pondering anything deeply. The main difference is that *now* you will be doing so more purposefully, with a goal in mind and some ancillary techniques that help improve the overall effect.

Meditation is very healthy, and it need not touch on spirituality issues. In fact, some of the meditation/visualization activities in this chapter have little to do with magick, per se. Witches know that true magick begins with a physically, mentally healthy self, one that is not always aware of and attuned to metaphysical energies—often because we're stressed or self-defeating in our outlooks.

Meditation is a key to rebuilding self-confidence and a positive image, which is essential to eventually becoming a fully activated Witch. Additionally, we have to learn to love ourselves again, no matter what residual teen-aged angst lingers in the back of our minds. If our magick isn't guided by a sure will and love, it's far more likely to go astray.

Before beginning, please read over each activity and make sure you're comfortable with it. No book or person can be the absolute authority for what form your personal quest for enlightenment should take. What I offer are guidelines at best.

You need to adjust and adapt each activity so it really makes sense to you. Any magickal procedure that has no meaning also has no power. Also, trusting that small positive voice within to guide and direct your path has to begin here and now, if it hasn't already. You don't need a guru; you are your own guru.

I do suggest that you note your reactions to each exercise that you try here in a magickal diary or journal that you maintain diligently. Read them over for insights periodically. You'll find doing so helps gauge growth, and it can actually become a foundation for a Book of Shadows later. For Witches, a Book of Shadows is a bible of sorts in which they find comfort, gather inspiration, and record good ideas for living a fulfilling magickal life every day.

Self-Images

Negative self-images are a difficult barrier for many of us to overcome. Humans are often personally critical, which in turn tears at the fibers of self-respect. The time for each spiritual seeker to reevaluate where their personal images originate is long overdue. Do they linger from childhood? Are they a result of family issues? Of culture? If you can identify the sources that are the root of self-doubt, it's much easier to pull that weed out of your conscious and subconscious mind.

If you don't know where a doubt or negative image originates, however, the process is a bit more difficult. You don't want to just be treating symptoms here, or the positive effects will be only temporary. The first step toward wholeness, then, is to examine your life honestly and find the source(s) of apprehension.

This can be a painful process, because a lot of memories often get dug up en route. The exercises in this chapter aren't quick fixes to rebuilding the self, a process that can take years—or even a lifetime. The more you can release the past, gathering its lessons and leaving the trash behind, the more effective the activities become. Like anything, your desire and determination to make a positive change directly influences how positive the results will be. These activities will help you learn to become your own best magickal friend.

ACTIVITY: Self-Evaluation

This exercise is reflective in nature. It should be done on a day when you don't have to rush, when you've had a good night's rest, and when your outlook is fairly balanced. Begin by finding a quiet place where you can write without interruptions. With two sheets of paper close by, sit down and take a few deep breaths.

Then, on the first sheet write all the things that you dislike about yourself. Be honest but fair. Then take out a second sheet, and list all your positive attributes. Don't forget to be fair to yourself here, too! Make sure both these lists look at all facets of your life: personal, professional, spiritual, playful, and so on. When you're done, put both pieces aside for a few minutes and just relax. Try to give yourself some emotional distance.

When you feel a little detached, read them as if they weren't about you at all, but about a friend. From this perspective some of the things you thought were horrible may suddenly seem less dramatic—or even really minor—compared to the good qualities. So what does this accomplish? Effectively, you have just realized that despite your shortcomings, you're a valuable human being.

Return your attention to the lists again. Mark on the "dislike" sheet all those things you feel you have the power and wherewithal to change. Put a target date next to that item. Please be realistic—lifelong habits won't disappear in a day, and if you're too impractical here you're liable to get discouraged. For example, if you're overweight, it's reasonable to *start* a healthy diet and exercise program immediately, but it's not reasonable to expect to look like a model after just one week! Similarly, there's nothing that says a few pounds here and there are "bad" unless they're harming you physically. Remember: Societal images have little in common with the sacred self that you're creating.

By the way, this writing activity is also very helpful when you face difficult decisions. You can make a sheet that represents each option at hand, list the advantages/disadvantages of each, and then review your lists to determine which one represents the most positive choice.

ACTIVITY: Embracing the God/dess Within

For this exercise you'll need a good-sized mirror (full-length if possible) that can be placed in a private room. You'll also need a god/dess image to which you relate intimately and positively. If you don't feel drawn to a particular aspect of the Divine, I suggest maybe a hero/ine instead, specifically one whose attributes are those after which you personally strive.

Wait until the moon is waxing (to support positive change), and take the image you've chosen to where the mirror is and put on some soft music. Make sure you feel wholly safe and comfortable in the atmosphere you're creating. Perhaps light a white candle for extra protection and peace.

Stand before the mirror fully clothed. Look at the wonder and beauty of your body. See how your eyes sparkle in the light, how your smile reflects joy to the shadows, what incredible tools you have in your arms, hands, and feet. As you do this slowly begin to undress. Drop the mundane world and related thoughts to the floor with each article of clothing. Release whatever they represent. Continue until you've stripped away all the exterior trappings that often constrain self-images.

Now, look at yourself in naked radiance. Don't shy away. Just because you may not match a physical ideal imposed by society doesn't mean you're not beautiful or handsome. And being naked certainly doesn't equate to some puritanical notion of evil. If these ideas hold you back, this is the time to try and overcome them—or at least make progress in that direction. Your body is sacred. Your flesh gently wraps around your soul and embraces your spirit, sustaining it, nurturing it, and giving it the medium through which to grow.

At this point, take out the image of the god/dess (or hero/ine) that you've brought with you. Concentrate on it until you can see it clearly in your mind's eye. Then sit on the floor in front of the mirror and look into your own eyes. Breathe slowly and evenly. In the center of your eye, visualize a tiny flame. This is the core of your being, vital and full of energy.

In that same flame, imagine the face of the god/dess you chose forming clearly. As you fill the flames with that image, also think of all the positive attributes represented by that persona. As you do, the flame and image will naturally grow larger and larger, filled with the glory of all that it is, and all that it can be. Slowly this will engulf you, being absorbed into your body and every portion of your being.

At some point you'll feel nearly ready to burst with energy and power. Open your eyes and look into the mirror at the face of the god/dess staring back at you! Look at your whole, shining being and know yourself as magickal. You are exactly what you were born to be. Accept this self with love and freedom.

When you're done, relax and slowly get dressed again. Write down your observations and feelings, noting especially how they differ from when you began. Repeat this exercise any time you need to purge an old, outworn view of self, or when you're not feeling overly sensual.

ACTIVITY: Free-Flow Writing

You'll need a notebook for this activity, a couple of pens (just in case one goes dry), a green candle (for creativity and growth), and perhaps some quiet instrumental music to put you in the right frame of mind. To begin, decide on one particular issue in your life (spiritual or mundane) on which to focus your attention, especially how you might ideally like things to change.

Next, light the candle stating your intention. For example, if you're trying to cool a frequently heated temper you might say, "I light this fire to remind me to be tolerant, patient, and

calm in the face of difficulty. Let its light shine peace in my life."
If you wish, you may also call upon the god/dess from the last
activity to bless and support your efforts for change at this time,
because the lit candle also represents Spirit's light.

As the candle burns, begin to write. Try not to think too
much, so you can focus all your energy on the matter at hand.
Consider why you get angry, what seems to trigger your temper,
and what you think might help keep that internal volcano under
control. Write until you feel you can write no more.

Put the pen down and rest a few minutes (you'll probably
feel a little tired anyway). Close your eyes and notice how much
tension and foreboding transferred from your body into the
paper through the writing process. It provides release and is
often quite liberating. After five or 10 minutes, return to what
you've written and read it. You'll likely find some very revealing
things here. We often know what's best for ourselves—the problem is finding the right tool to access that information!

For readers who find writing isn't the best medium for
expression, try painting, carving, or orating and see what you
come up with! Remember, no one else has to see your free-flow
work, so it need not be artistically grand. This is for your eyes
only. On a similar note, magickal artists who experience a creative block often find this exercise or an adaptation thereto helpful in overcoming that obstacle.

Finally, keep the candle handy. Light it any time you
notice yourself getting hot under the collar so it can release calming energy into the room and symbolize the light of reason.

ACTIVITY: Bandage and Heal

Witches with gaping holes in their psyche due to past
struggles often find it hard to direct their metaphysical energy
effectively. This visualization activity is designed as an astral bandage that you can place over the wounds left behind when life's
wheel runs over you or when you feel downtrodden or frustrated.

I recommend trying this from the comfort of a warm tub, where you can really separate yourself from outside influences. Add a bundle of chamomile and lavender to the water as aromatherapy for peace and tranquility. Light some personally pleasing incense, and place a candle on the tub while you soak. As you lay in the water, release your tensions and worries into the warmth.

When you feel more centered and calm, close your eyes and see yourself somewhere that has always made you feel safe and secure. Include a trusted friend in the imagery. As that person walks into the picture, you notice he or she is carrying an oversized bandage that looks warm and comforting.

As your friend gets closer and wraps you in this bandage, giving you a much-needed hug, you experience total, unconditional love and healing energy. Stay in this safe cocoon until you feel your depression lifting and your energy returning. (Note that in serious cases of despondency you may have to repeat the visualization several times for it to result in quantifiable changes.)

One word of caution: Avoid this activity if you're overly tired. Falling asleep in the bathtub is not going to help the healing process!

The Power in Your Name

I mentioned earlier that names have power. If you don't think this is true, watch what happens when you (or anyone) mispronounces or misspells someone's name. Part of this reaction comes from the ego wishing to be recognized, to feel important and worthy. Another part of the reaction has to do with the fact that a name designates the entirety of our being from the time of our birth onward.

Our names are very important. These activities work to strengthen the magickal connection to our given names and to help in choosing spiritual names to empower and shape our future paths.

ACTIVITY: Affirming Your Birth Name

Do you like your name? Why or why not? People who don't like their name often don't like themselves either. Alternatively, there might be some negative connotation to this name that comes from your personal experiences, either in this life or in past lives. No matter what the situation, you need to resolve the feelings you have toward your given name before you can consider choosing a magickal one.

One way to do this is by looking at the origins and meanings for your name. For example, I've never really liked being called Patricia (thus the nickname Trish). But when I discovered that it means "noble" or "peacemaker," I was kind of excited. I've always been somewhat of a gentle soul, seeking peace wherever it could be made. Somehow I have to believe that my birth name helped shape this part of my personality.

When I stumbled across this information, I tried an affirmation exercise. I went to a private spot and declared my name to the winds with these statements: "I am Patricia. There is power in my name." and "I am Patricia, who can make and find peace."

Try this yourself. Feel the strength in the name that has been with you for so long. Sing your name, draw it, whisper it to the winds, and let them carry a blessing back to you.

To adapt this activity for a coven or study group, have each person in the group take turns standing in the center of your circle. The entire group then chants that person's name while each member in turn shares something positive about the individual. For example, if the member's name is Frank, then everyone repeats the name Frank rhythmically. While this goes on, one person might say "Frank is generous." Then, other members in turn add their positive observations. Most people find this activity very uplifting.

ACTIVITY: Finding and Using a Magickal Name

At a Witch's initiation (and sometimes even before that) the seeker chooses a new name. This represents the end of one cycle (the one connected to the flesh) and the beginning of a new life of spirit and magick. Exactly how you choose this name can vary. You could take it from a cultural tradition you're following (Greek, Egyptian, whatever). Or you might look to mythology for a positive role model. Whatever your choice, this name should represent the best of what you are, and all that you hope to become through your Witchcraft.

After selecting a name, you might want to consider holding a naming ritual for yourself, where you'll share this name with the Universe and the Sacred Powers. (I recommend you do research on names and discuss with people in your magickal community prior to conducting this ritual.) For my naming ritual, I created an area where pictures and symbols from my past were on one side of the circle. On the other side of the circle I placed magickal tools and symbols of what I hoped to achieve by following this path.

At some point in your personal ritual, take up only those things from the past that you feel were positive. Leave the rest behind. Turn away from that area of the sacred space and move to the other side. Pick up the items waiting for you there, and speak your magickal name out loud. Do this four times, once to each Quarter (East, South, North, and West, moving clockwise). If you wish, this is also a good time to declare your desire to cultivate mystical knowledge and wisdom to the Powers and ask for their aid.

Although you're likely to continue using your given name every day, this new name will prove powerful in ritual and spellcraft. In magickal groups, many people adopt their magickal name as a nickname so the resonance of that name's energy is with them more frequently.

Outmoded Habits and Views

When we were children we thought and spoke as children. As we grow into spiritual maturity, however, our childhood perceptions and ways don't often fit the new reality. Even as adults we experience many shifts and surprises that cause us to reevaluate old ways of thinking, acting, and being, including some habits, attitudes, and ideas we've acquired over the years. At this juncture we often discover (or rediscover) a deep-seeded desire for change. The following activities are designed to help you achieve the process of change.

ACTIVITY: A Flowering Spell

An old folk spell begins with gathering the seed from a flowering plant that somehow represents the transformation you wish to make in yourself. For example, if you don't feel you're loving enough, a rose might suit. Name this seed of self after what you're trying to cultivate in place of the negative attribute, and then plant it in rich soil. Set the plant in a nice sunny window and tend it lovingly. Repeat the word that represents your goal each time you tend the plant.

While you tend the plant of self, also begin making honest efforts on a tangible level to bring about the desired change. Witches know that magick matches energy for energy. Effort, when combined with intention, always results in the most powerful spells.

When the plant first shows signs of sprouting you should also begin noticing a change in yourself. By the time it flowers, your desire should be answered (but not always as you expect). Sometimes we have to accept and work through things because that's what's best for us. In any case, the sight of that flower should continue to give you strength for the task ahead.

ACTIVITY: Realizing the Power of Perspective

In order to change our actions or thoughts we first have to get a different perspective on them. I often find it difficult to make a transformation if I have no idea where or why a problem originally developed. In some ways it's like closing the proverbial barn door after the horses get loose! When you find yourself in similar situations, this meditation may help.

Begin by breathing slowly and evenly. Those of you who have practiced magick for awhile know the natural effect this has on your body, mind, and spirit, bringing all three into a focused harmony. When you find yourself at ease, turn your thoughts to that idea or habit that you want to change. This time, however, rather than being an active participant in that situation, become an observer. Think of it as if it was a mental movie theater. (Make popcorn if it helps.)

Now watch as things unfold. Say, for example, you can't figure out why you seem to always be short on time. In the visualization you might observe your whole day from start to finish, noting instances of procrastination, distraction, and disorganization. Once you understand and acknowledge what turns your attention away from the tasks or goals at hand, you can begin avoiding those types of situations or better handling them.

ACTIVITY: Repatterning the Past

Since magick works forward and backward in time, there is distinct potential in enacting visualizations that return us to the past, and then repatterning that past in order to positively affect the present or future. Before you try this activity, think of a symbol that represents one thing from the past that you'd like to transform in yourself. Also, set up a protected space in which to work. Think of it like locking your doors when you leave home— only in this case the doors are astral ones. Whatever energies or beings you don't want to allow in, stay firmly outside.

If you're not familiar with the process, the easiest way to make your body a sacred space unto itself is by seeing yourself in a bubble of silvery white light. The surface of this bubble is reflective so as to turn back unwanted influences. Inside, your magickal energy stays neatly in place for you to work with until you disperse the visualization!

After creating your protected space, sit down in an area where you won't be disturbed. See yourself in your mind's eye as you sit right now. Once that image is secure, slowly begin turning back the hands of time so you see yourself at progressively younger ages. (It may help to look through an old scrapbook or photo album beforehand so you remember these images easily.) When you reach the age when you felt fairly responsible for your decisions, stop.

Bring an image of yourself as an adult into the portrait. Have the adult you walk up to the younger you and paint or draw the symbol you've chosen on the youth's third eye. Do this three times: once here, the second time at a slightly older age, and the third time moving forward into the future a few more years (past your current age). This effectively surrounds the present with magick from both time lines, as patterned by your own mind and heart.

Repeat this activity as necessary to help you reach your goals, and make notes of the results in your magickal journal.

Developing Awareness

A natural by-product of changing the way we think about ourselves is a transformation in our awareness: of self, of others, of the Earth. Magick depends heavily on intuitive senses for guidance. So, developing this awakened, aware state is a tremendous aid to magickal living today.

Part of this process includes prioritizing and broadening our horizons. It's always important to know what's most important to making our dreams realities, while still tending to the day-to-day responsibilities. From this perspective, it's much easier to see how our action (or inaction) affects the web of life. This awareness then will help us adjust to rapidly changing times and tailor our magick to include more global objectives.

ACTIVITY: Observing from All Directions

This simple exercise will work with almost any object, although a faceted crystal seems to work best because it has several angles/sides. Take your chosen object and place it on a table in front of you against a plain, dark cloth. Look at it somewhat casually. What's its aesthetic value? Where is it in relationship to other objects in the room, including yourself?

Next, move the crystal slightly in any direction. Build on your original observations, but notice now how the light strikes it differently, and how the color shifts a bit due to its new location. Going one step further, look at each of the crystal's facets as it relates to the room. How are the colors and textures visually changed by the facet's placement? Compare this information to your original observations.

By now you probably have a clear picture of this crystal in your mind. Pick it up and close your eyes. See it in your mind's eye and feel it in your hand. Reach out all your senses and get to know the natural spirit that resides there. Again, note your experience and compare it to earlier observations.

At the end of this exercise, do you find that you appreciate it more or understand its basic energy matrix better for having looked at it this way? Most people find that they do. While it may feel a little silly to sit and play with a crystal, this particular exercise is retraining your mind to be more observant on all levels, to focus on all facets of a situation, and gather information effectively. It is an admirable skill to learn, not only for Witches, but for anyone who truly wants to know how to walk a mile in someone else's shoes, or be able to discern more than the superficials in any circumstance.

ACTIVITY: Sensual Centering

This activity will enable you to heighten your senses so you can learn to direct them for insight and/or information.

You'll need to work with a partner, someone with whom you have a good rapport and who is sensitive to your energy. This individual should also have a pleasing voice and the ability to get creative with guided meditations. If you cannot find such a person, you can pre-record this activity for yourself. You'll also need a gong or bell handy.

Take the time to center yourself and breathe deeply. Your partner will wait and recite a word or phrase when he or she notices you're moving into a meditative state. Following that word or phrase, he or she rings the bell, which creates a sound upon which to focus and which inspires inner harmony. Just as the last echo of the bell fades, your guide will recite another short word or phrase upon which to focus. This should give you plenty of time to integrate the associated energy.

Here are some examples of the phrases you can use in this exercise to awaken your senses and focus on their power:

SEE FOREVER IN YOUR CLOSED EYES. [bell rings, then fades]

VISUALIZE BREATH AS LIGHT THAT FILLS YOUR BEING.

CONSIDER THE SOUND OF SILENCE.

LISTEN TO THE MUSIC OF YOUR SOUL.

HEAR THE SONG OF TIME AS IT WHISPERS OF PAST LIVES.

SENSE THE DRUMMING OF YOUR HEARTBEAT.

FEEL THE AIR AS IT CARESSES YOUR SKIN.

BECOME ONE WITH THE MOVEMENTS OF THE EARTH BENEATH YOU.

DISCERN THE TEXTURE OF YOUR OWN AURA.

TASTE THE SALT OF THE SEA IN THE WIND.

SAVOR THE FLAVOR OF WHITE, CLEANSING LIGHT.

TASTE THE FRESH WATER IN YOUR WELL OF CREATIVITY.

INHALE THE STRENGTH OF THE EARTH INTO YOUR BODY.

SMELL THE PERFUME OF PEACE AS IT SETTLES ON YOUR SPIRIT.

BREATHE THE COLORS OF THE RAINBOW FOR RENEWED HOPE.

ACTIVITY: Awakening the Senses

After creating an appropriate magickal space within which to work, you can use invocation as a means to awaken your senses and bring them into full awareness.

As you recite the invocation it helps to light an appropriate colored candle for each part: yellow for Air, green for Earth, red for Fire, and blue for Water. It also helps to have some soil, water, a fan, and perhaps some burning incense to represent each sense and give you a specific focal point upon which to place your attention. As you recite each portion of the invocation, light the corresponding candle and touch the element somehow. (Note: Get close enough to the heat generated by your incense to awaken the fire, but not get burned by it.)

Some of my students have said that playing a tape or CD with nature sounds heightens the effect of this invocation.

You'll notice that I've included a sixth part to this invocation for the self. It is in *you* that all the Elements come together for Witchcraft, producing the wonderful essence of magick.

Air: I WELCOME THE SENSE OF SMELL—THE WARM FRESH SCENTS OF A SPRING WIND THAT CHANTS A MAGICKAL SONG AND FILLS ME WITH HOPE. [Light a white or yellow candle. Go to a window or fan and feel the wind, or breathe very deeply.]

Fire: I WELCOME THE SENSE OF SIGHT—THE VISION THAT COMES WHEN HEAVENLY FIRES FILL THE EARTH AND RENEW MY ENERGY, PASSION, AND POWER. [Light a red or orange candle. Get close to something warm, or pay particular attention to your body heat.]

Water: I WELCOME THE SENSE OF TASTE—THAT POURS FROM THE SEAS AND SKY INTO MY SPIRIT WITH INSIGHT AND HEALING. [Light a blue candle. Sprinkle yourself with a little water or drink a glass of spring water to internalize that energy.]

Earth: I WELCOME THE SENSE OF TOUCH—THAT BEGINS IN THE EARTH BENEATH MY FEET AND ANCHORS MY SOUL. [Light a green candle. Run your fingers through some rich soil.]

Spirit: I WELCOME THE SENSE OF HEARING—THAT RESOUNDS WITH TRUTH AND AWARENESS, OFFERING PERSPECTIVE. [Light a white candle. Listen closely for anything—your heartbeat, your breath, a noise, whatever.]

Self: I EMPOWER ALL MY SENSES, FLOWING FROM THE OCEAN AND REACHING TO THE STARS, AND THE SILENT WEAVE OF TIME AND SPACE THAT GUIDES MY MAGICK. [If you wish, light a candle that's your favorite color to represent self. Open your arms to the universe and welcome its energy.]

Banishing Fear and Blockage

Fear is a very inhibiting emotion that strangles and stagnates our attempts at individual expression and magickal exploration. Blockage often works similarly in that when we get frustrated there's a temptation to give up, turn around, and walk away from that wall. These two exercises are designed to help you overcome those suppressive fears and surmount the walls that stand in your way of progressing along the Path of Beauty.

ACTIVITY: Turning Fear Inside Out

I imagine fear as a cloudy black figure produced by dwelling on negative thoughts. When I name that figure (fear of flying, fear of vulnerability, fear of failure, or whatever fear it may be), I then grab that image by the shoulders in my meditation/visualization and turn it inside out like a pair of socks. Sure enough, inside that cloud is a bright shining being, filled with confidence (because fear reversed becomes security).

If you feel this imagery will work for you, try it with one specific phobia. Note your feelings before and after the meditation. It's very important, however, that you remember to name your shadow. Knowing something's name gives you power over it (in this case the power to turn things around)!

ACTIVITY: Breaking Down Brick Walls

The brick walls in this activity can represent problems, fears, or obstacles. I should mention before sharing this activity that some walls in our life have a purpose. Consider the one you're struggling with closely. It might be too soon to proceed with this activity, or you might need to consider things more fully before charging forward.

On the other hand, when you feel there's a useless barrier in your way, then you can try this visualization as a way of wheedling away the energy-impeding progress. Begin with an image of a huge brick wall in your mind. As with the previous activity, you must name this wall. Perhaps see yourself painting the name of what it represents on the bricks along with all the associated feelings you have toward this situation. Be specific.

Now, take a moment and back up from your wall. This will give you some perspective. Make sure you're not missing a perfect alternative to going around the wall on the left or the right. Very often we're so close to our walls that other options elude us. This is your chance to possibly find an easier route.

Should there be no other way, then look down. There's a hammer on the ground next to you. Pick it up and begin pounding at the wall. It may take some time to make a crack, but that is progress—even little cracks let the light of hope through. Continue until you make a hole big enough for you to step through, and do just that! You are now on the other side of the wall. Look around and see what awaits you there.

Repeating this exercise improves its effects. Just making a hole in the wall doesn't mean it can't close up again, so you may need to duplicate your meditation. Many people find that this particular imagery is powerful for helping the body's natural healing process. They name the wall after an illness and then take a hammer to that sickness. If the person feels they made progress in the meditation, the body's immune system seems strengthened by the effort.

Anger and Blame

Two other destructive forms of energy, anger and blame, can fester inside even the most ardent of Witches and create spiritual cancers that are hard to clear away. These astral dis-eases taint our magick, so it's important to make an honest effort to banish them. There's enough negativity surrounding us in today's world without such darkness gnawing at our spirits. These exercises may help.

ACTIVITY: Channeling Anger I

I don't always deal with my anger in constructive ways. My gut instinct flares up and wants to physically or verbally express my ire. I suspect I'm not alone in this, and although I'm not an advocate of always biting your tongue (this causes ulcers) there *are* positive ways of channeling anger so that you can handle a situation with your head on straight.

Find something breakable that you don't mind smashing. Go outside and hold it in both hands. Pour all your fury into that object. Let the anger build steadily until you can't help but vehemently throw the object to the ground, which should shatter it—symbolically breaking apart your anger. This also physically disengages the anger and pushes it away.

Carefully collect these shards and consider using them for a Witch Bottle or other magick aimed at turning mal-intended spells. Alternatively, bury the shards in the ground and plant something that flowers above the pieces (these act as a drainage system). This way anger will continue to "drain away" while something positive grows in its place.

You should now be calm enough to handle the situation far more effectively.

ACTIVITY: Channeling Anger II

There are other ways to channel your anger, too. On a very mundane level, take a walk, go for a run, or try primal screams. The energy of these activities releases a lot of pent-up aggression. You can also try to pour your anger into an artistic medium, such as painting or sculpting, then ritually destroy it afterward so you can watch the anger disappear. The result is the same as with the previous activity: You should now be calmer and ready to handle the situation.

ACTIVITY: Casting a Forgiveness Spell

When anger has torn at the very fibers of your being and bitterness is rooted therein, use your magick to help the healing process begin. If your difficulty is toward a particular person, it helps if they're willing to participate in this spell with you, but you can do it alone to open the way for forgiveness. (If the other person is willing to do a forgiveness spell with you, then have him or her follow this process at the same time as you, or even in the same place, so you can have a clean slate afterward.)

You'll need to place a piece of white cloth and an item on the altar that represents the problem at hand. You'll also need a red candle, a white candle, and a blue candle, for love, peace, and understanding, respectively. Consider doing this when the moon is new, to mark a fresh start. Alternatively, a waning moon can encourage "shrinking" anger.

Go to the altar and light the candles, speaking their purpose (peace, love, understanding) aloud as you touch flame to the wick. Next, pick up the object and pour your feelings into that object. Conjure up mental imagery to bring that situation back into focus. Continue pouring out your feelings until the object feels physically hot. Then wrap it in white cloth while whispering the word "forgiveness" three times into the bundle.

Blow out your candles and take the object to a place where you can burn, bury, or otherwise safely dispose of it to symbolically put the anger away from you. Turn your back and walk away. Do not look back.

By the way, this spell may be adapted for ridding yourself of guilt, but in this case substitute a poppet that resembles yourself in place of the object (because in this case, the thing that needs forgiveness is *you*).

◆ ◆ ◆

Many challenges await us as Witches in the new millennium. At least one challenge is what we accept as truth for our lives from the people around us or society. The old saying "you are what you eat" has a lot of bearing on this challenge. We can consume the garbage randomly portrayed in various media that generates hate, prejudice, misconceptions, and the like, or we can choose a more positive way—the way of meditation and thoughtfulness.

On a similar note, we don't live neatly sequestered away from our communities where nothing affects us. The bad vibes that often linger in everyday life aren't always easy to detect, let alone shake off. People scatter their emotional and psychic baggage all over the place, usually without knowing it, and spiritually sensitive people often pick this up without knowing it, either.

If you find times when you feel depressed or out of sorts for no reason, give yourself some magickal downtime. Just as a good physician washes up before seeing a patient, remember that *you* are your most important patient. Find a way to maintain your spiritual hygiene. You might try a magickal bath to which purifying herbs are added, such as pine, or smudging yourself with sage smoke regularly. These efforts—and other similar ones—will keep your aura free of residual energies that increase tension, hinder focused meditations, and deter free-flowing magick.

Chapter 2

Talking the Talk

A superior man is modest in his speech, but exceeds in his actions.

—Confucious

The inner struggle that occurs with change is difficult. Harder still are the ways in which internal and external changes affect our relationships, our roles in society, our homes, and our circles. The world has been transforming very quickly in recent years, leaving many people lost or confused in the shuffle. This means that it is more important than ever for spiritually minded folk to strengthen our bonds. We need to share fellowship, and exchange ideas, as well as gather some semblance of coherency from one another.

To do this four factors must co-exist: tolerance, trust, good communication skills, and sensitivity. Unfortunately, more often than not, our fear of becoming vulnerable or getting involved in group dynamics hinders positive, honest exchanges. Be that as it may, Witches need to make a place for ourselves—

and indeed for all people, by way of example—to step outside the boundaries of complacency and dare to be different. Where need exits, we should follow the example of the ancient cunning folk and extend a helping hand. When we're hurting, we should likewise open up and ask for assistance and support.

I admit this is tough. It requires nothing less than teaching ourselves entirely new ways of interacting with each other. But that's really what the New Age asks of us. To shake off the preconceived notions. To stop perceiving acts of compassion or confession as illustrating weakness and shame. To sail away from the aloof island and reach out beyond ourselves. The rewards for stretching ourselves and our magick will prove more than worthwhile. It will help us rediscover and build our "tribes."

When I use the word *tribe*, I mean that group of people who are truly family, even if they are not related to you. In magickal traditions the tribe is very important. These are people to whom you can go anytime—day or night—for advice, help, or just company. As tribes are founded on trust, that is where this chapter must begin.

The Adventure of Trust

I find it interesting to see that trusting others also requires me to trust myself and my instincts. Whether I'm having coffee with a friend, helping at a ritual, or standing in a crowded elevator, the choice to reach out—or not—lies heavily with my inner voice (and whether or not I stop to listen to that voice).

Another factor in the whole trust equation seems to be what society considers proper. Much to the disconcertion of Emily Post, our needs don't always recognize what's "proper" in the public eye. Yet, we find ourselves often hesitating to offer a kind gesture for fear of reproach and misunderstanding. What would happen if we didn't stop—if those "random" acts of kindness started happening anytime, anywhere?

I think the answer is that we would feel relief. When people discover their common humanity without pretense or the need for appearances, it releases a lot of tension. It's easy to get caught up in the workaday mode and overlook opportunities to tune in, reach out, and make a difference.

ACTIVITY: Listening to Yourself

Before you can really tune into other people's energies and words, you need to become more aware of your own. Words have tremendous power to heal or hurt—not only others, but yourself. For this activity you really need only two good ears and the ability to remain attentive to your own conversations. Ask yourself the following questions:

- **Are my words positive and life affirming?** If not, start consciously making changes in the way you present ideas. Instead of stressing a negative, turn the idea around and find the positive—especially when speaking about yourself.

- **Am I putting myself down frequently?** If so, refer to the first point here. Go back to Chapter One and add a few of those exercises into your weekly routine to bolster self-confidence.

- **Do I share my opinions in a beneficial manner?** Especially in magick, there's no need to prove rightness or wrongness, even if it's tempting. Always try to share with wisdom, expressing convictions in a healthy manner rather than condemning or criticizing. By so doing you can generate a wonderful type of magick: understanding!

- **Am I quick to accept other people's opinions about my personal welfare?** This is what I call the guru syndrome—you feel so unsure you're tempted to accept input from nearly any source about what's right for your life. In magick, this is very dangerous and not helpful to your spiritual goals at all. You are always the best voice of reason for decisions affecting your own life. Get opinions, yes, but balance them against what you feel in your heart.

♦ **Do I bite my tongue on matters that are important to me?** Internalizing opinions and emotions that might be best let out can cause physical illness, so be aware of that. The trick is learning to express those ideas constructively. Note: This guideline is true for those times when people hurt your feelings, too. You can't hold someone liable for pain if they didn't know what they said is painful!

♦ **Am I sharing this information just to be involved in a conversation?** There are times to speak and times to be silent. Wisdom comes in knowing the difference. In any conversation someone has to listen for another person to be heard.

♦ **Am I speaking clearly and in an organized manner?** This question goes back to the old saying "be sure your brain is in gear before shifting your tongue to high!" I can't tell you how many times I've suffered from foot-in-mouth syndrome. This could have easily been avoided by stopping just long enough to consider my words, their intentions, and the way they might be perceived.

These points may seem mundane, but no one ever said that our rationality need be lost in the pursuit of true magick. Re-creating our lives to mirror Wiccan ideals and practices begins within so it can be expressed without, and this includes our logical selves.

ACTIVITY: Fine-Tuning Your Perception of Others

Once you're more aware of the way you communicate with people, you can redirect your attention to improving your awareness and understanding of others. This activity focuses on learning how to see beyond the surface of what people say.

I suggest you go to an area where you can simply listen to several people at once without interacting (a shopping mall, for example). Consider each of these individuals as if he or she was a symphony of music. The intent of their words plays all around them, throughout their auric envelope. To "hear" this music, take a deep breath and put yourself in a semi-meditative state, then focus in on one individual. Do his or her words sound like a quiet brook or a blazing fire? Are they elusive like the wind or sensible and grounded like Earth?

If you're someone who relates to textures more strongly than sound, consider the nap and grain of the words instead. Are they like silk, bumpy, sticky, itchy? All these sensations are very telling with regard to a person's intention. The smooth, gentle discourse is often relaxed and honest, the rough and bumpy is angry or irritated, and the itchy can indicate lies or serious social discomfort. Some other indicators include:

- ◆ **Dishonesty:** pasty, static, or bitter tasting.
- ◆ **Irritation:** coarse, crunchy, or displeasing.
- ◆ **Love:** slightly sticky, warm, sweet.
- ◆ **Sincerity:** cool (not cold), constant, or refreshing.

After a little practice you'll be able to activate this awareness in a variety of settings. By so doing you'll have a better idea of those individuals with whom you can have positive discourse on any number of subjects, not just magick. I think the everyday Witch will find this ability particularly helpful at the office, where politics and group dynamics often interfere with perception. It's also very useful in determining what spiritual groups or covens might be right for you.

ACTIVITY: Determining the Animal/Element Within

Our language is very telling with regard to personality. We often speak of a calm, nurturing person or think of the proverbial green-thumb type as earthy. We describe people as eating like birds and being as cunning as cats or as faithful as dogs. What would happen if you took this idea into the astral realm? Discovering another person's Element or animal persona could help you understand your feelings toward them better.

How would knowing this help in the everyday working world? Say you met a new supervisor and immediately felt uncomfortable with him or her. You could enact the following exercise and try to comprehend that odd feeling. For example, Fire people are pretty antsy around Water people. Similarly, if you're an astral cat and your supervisor has a strong dog-type personality, there's a natural nervous reaction to anticipate here. While most folks have a blend of several characteristics in their personality, one will dominate, and it's to that domineering trait that we often react, even unwittingly.

For this activity, you'll need to be able to sit (or stand) a fair distance from the individual in question. As you look at him or her, try not to look at anything specific. In fact, let your vision blur slightly. Breathe, relax, keep watching, and mentally focus on your intention. As you do, you should begin to see an image, colors, patterns, or a symbol of the person appear in the haze. Make a mental note of what you see and consider it later when mulling over your feelings.

Dark colors often indicate depression, pessimism, or anxiety. Bright clear colors frequently indicate health or happiness. Symbols will vary by what those emblems mean to you (you can use a dream or divination dictionary, such as my *The Language of Dreams,* to help interpret these). Animals represent strong personality traits. For example, a dog is loyal, but sometimes also very territorial. Bear in mind, however, that this is a broad generalization. Ultimately trust your instincts. Your spiritual self will always give you information in a form that makes sense to you.

I've personally found this activity very helpful in tense situations, especially when I'm working with a new group or counseling someone while I'm on the road. This is a great coping mechanism that at least explains apprehensions that seem to have no foundation, even though they do in the spiritual realm.

Solo Interaction

You've learned to listen to yourself and be more attentive to other's auric messages and the true meaning in their communications. The next logical step is opening the door to more in-depth interactions and walking through! Work one-on-one with people to further develop your communication skills on all levels (physical, mental, and spiritual).

I'm a great advocate of taking small steps forward, and you're less likely to put on airs with just one person than with a group (and vice versa). Experience has shown me that if you're going to learn to talk effectively about spiritual matters, the greatest learning experiences often happen on a one-to-one basis. It is for these very reasons that I've spent a little extra time and space on this subject here. If you can't master interaction with one person, being successful with groups or covens is going to be really tough.

There are some rules of conversation to follow that will help tremendously. First, always maintain good eye contact. It shows interest and honesty. If you have trouble with direct eye contact, try looking just past the person to a point on the wall.

Second, don't rush your words. Speak clearly, presenting your ideas in a manner that reflects thoughtfulness, enthusiasm, or whatever is appropriate. If you have a habit of tapping your fingers, jiggling your knee, or other nervous tendencies, be aware of and try to stop them. They'll distract from your intention and make your companion aware of your tension or nervousness, which might be misconstrued.

Finally, share the conversation. Don't domineer or be overly demure. Keep your spiritual ears open along with other intuitive senses. Speak with honesty, respect, and consideration, and your discourse will show tremendous changes for the better, no matter the subject.

ACTIVITY: Musing Magickally

Get together with a friend who shares your interest in Wicca or magick. Sit together and pick a topic for discussion. Next, breathe in a slow, rhythmic manner that matches one another. This helps get you in sync with each other's energy levels and will mingle your auric spheres a bit.

Continue the rhythmic breathing for about five minutes before you start talking about the chosen topic. Most people find that they naturally know when to speak, when to listen, at least part of what their partner is going to say, and when to end the discussion. It flows from beginning to end. When you reach the point where the discussion has ended, ground yourselves out.

ACTIVITY: Combatting Busy Signals

This spell is specifically designed to open the lines of communication between yourself and another when you feel that something (or someone) hinders that discourse. It basically sends out a welcoming message. Whether or not this person is willing to answer the invitation remains up to him or her.

Begin with a length of string, perhaps yellow in color to augment the energy of communication, long enough so that paper and string can stretch across the table. You also need a yellow candle; a piece of paper about three square inches with the person's name on it; and a blend of allspice, apple peel, clove, dandelion, and pine as incense. Just a pinch or two foster friendship, peace, kinship, welcoming, and clearing, respectively. If you have another incense that represents these things to you, by all means use it!

Light the incense and the candle. Take the piece of paper with the name written on it and fold it in half three times. Wrap this with one end of the string, tying it with three knots. Put this across the table from you and keep the other end of the string in your hand. The candle should be in the middle of the table.

Think about all the things you would say to this person if you could. Send that message out along the thread. As you do, slowly draw the bundle closer to you until it rests in your hand. This symbolically closes the gap between you and that person.

Burn the paper with the incense to release your prayers and wishes to the four winds. Take the remnants and scatter them outside as part of the message spell so each breeze speaks of your hospitality.

An alternative approach to this spell is carrying the paper with you after it comes to rest in your hand. Each time you touch the paper, think about your message. Keep it with you until communications open again, and then burn it in thankfulness.

This activity is a great way to encourage a letter or phone call from a loved one who you haven't heard from in a long time.

ACTIVITY: Motivating Positive Interactions

Communicating with people you don't like is difficult, especially difficult if that person is in your coven, part of your department at work, or regularly part of your daily routine in some other way. But have you ever noticed that if you give people a gentle, nurturing, positive nudge or redirection, that person's demeanor changes for the better, thereby improving your ability to communicate?

For this activity pick someone with whom you dread interacting. Find one characteristic of that person that you can appreciate—even if it's only his or her taste in socks! Go out of your way to be cooperative, uplifting, considerate, and polite. Give this activity a fair chance to work (at least a week). Nearly every time I've tried this, it manifests enough of a change to make the uncomfortable situation bearable.

People, when properly motivated and appreciated, can—and do—change if we give them a chance. This won't work 100 percent of the time, but building up others honestly and gently also bolsters the positive energy in and around the places where you work, play, and live, benefiting everyone.

ACTIVITY: Extending a Magickal Touch

A lot of people, including myself, are hung up on touch. They're hesitant or uncomfortable about reaching out even with just a hand on someone's shoulder. This likely stems from various sources: our puritanical heritage, our insecurities about our bodies, the fear of misunderstanding, and a concern about violating personal space. Be that as it may, science has shown us that touch is not only important to our communicative process, but also to our development as people. In turn, this would suggest it is also important to our development as Witches.

The gentle touch of a hand or a hug can often express what might take three hours to convey otherwise. In today's world we're all time-challenged. Breaching the touch barrier helps create "quality" where "quantity" might not be possible. How do you begin? Slowly.

Work with a friend or loved one where trust already exists. Start embracing your friends when you greet them and when you say good-bye to them. Place a hand on someone's arm when you're talking about deeply important or personal matters. Your aura can communicate worlds of meaning through that touch. You might also consider gentle shoulder massages as a way of getting past the touch barrier. Ask first, but almost everyone appreciates them—and you can talk while you work! I think you'll find the conversation automatically becomes more relaxed and intimate because of that contact.

ACTIVITY: Controlling Your Aura

How often have you worked with a novice Witch who had little or no control over his or her personal energy? This activity is designed to help with that, and to continue to build your own regulatory systems. Better still, the natural by-product of this exercise is a deepening awareness of another person's auric envelope, which is always handy.

Start by sitting knee-to-knee with your partner. Place your hands palm down over your partner's, whose are palm up. Your hands should have about a quarter-inch gap between them. Both of you should now focus all your attention and energy on your hands. Feel the heat being generated there. This is a physical manifestation of two auras in such close proximity (actually overlapping at this moment). Visualize this heat as light shining from between the hands.

Slowly start moving your hands apart, but keep the energy constant. Always remain actively aware of your energy and that of your partner's so the resulting bundle of energy stays uniform. When your hands are about six inches apart, stop. You now have a good sized light-ball of auric energy between the two of you. When you get really good at this activity you can actually play catch with this energy ball, or make two and let them break over one another to bathe your auras in trust. Alternatively, both partners can turn their hands downward to the Earth to ground the energy and bless the planet.

Group Interaction

The phrase "group dynamics" sends shivers down my back. It conjures up all kinds of mental images, many of them unpleasant, which is why I've been a loner most of my life. Be that as it may, in magickal groups each person must be trusted for responsible use of his or her energy. This means that we have to deal with the dynamic issues in creative ways, especially in our busy world, where each person likely has dramatically different needs, time constraints, and so on.

Before addressing the spiritual aspect, let's look at some points that contribute to effective group communications:

♦ **Never assume that people automatically understand what you're saying.** This is incredibly important when discussing magickal methods, where the success of any process depends heavily on comprehension and meaningfulness.

♦ **Make suggestions.** A group is only as great as the sum of its parts. The more each person participates and shares, the greater the coherency of the whole.

♦ **Respond positively.** Just as you would wish your ideas to be heard and considered seriously, return the favor. Even if modifications come out of the discourse, each opinion is valid and should be expressed without fear of being brushed off.

♦ **Participate regularly.** It's very hard to maintain groups where people are constantly dropping in and out of the Circle. This will mean taking a little extra time in the planning process to find the best dates suited to most people's schedules, but it's worth the effort.

Along the same lines, if some of your members have children, consider setting up a rotating or cooperative babysitting service so that everyone can attend adult rituals without undue financial strain.

♦ **Accept new members judiciously.** In magick more is not always better. You need not automatically open your doors to everyone who thinks he or she wants to join your group. I suggest instead offering a trial period during which the individual and the group see if they mingle positively. At the end of this period the group can make a determination whether or not to accept that person as a permanent member.

Note: In some circles the traditional training period before someone can become initiated as a full member is a year and a day. However, most people will know long before that time whether or not the spiritual relationship between members is going to work or not.

♦ **Release members without disdain.** Wicca grows and changes with each person in unique ways. In some cases this leads an individual to seek out a different path or group with whom to work. Don't see this as an insult. Instead, celebrate the progress of your fellow Witch, and wish him or her well on the Path of Beauty he or she chooses.

♦ **Follow the lines of authority.** If your group has a distinct leader, use that person's wisdom to help sort out difficult situations. Go to him or her with problems, questions, and worries. The leader was given this role for a reason, but can do little if the group's members don't avail themselves of the resource.

These basic rules will build strong bonds between group members, mostly due to common courtesy. Unlike many churches, each member of your group is not just a warm body filling a seat. Each person is important to the functioning of the whole, and any magick created.

Here are some magickal activities to help improve communications in groups and keep the spiritual energies fresh, vital, and alive.

ACTIVITY: Bonding Within Your Group

This exercise is excellent for a study group or a coven. It will teach you about how others perceive you—and how you perceive them. To begin, the group breathes in unison, guided by the leader. Matching your breathing patterns helps encourage a harmony in the auric fields of everyone present.

Next, each person in turn thinks of a positive phrase to describe other members of the circle. What is it that strikes you most about them? For example, you might start with Mike, saying, "Mike is joyful." The next person in the circle is Mary, who you've always seen as a peacemaker, so you might say, "Mary brings composure." Continue this way around the entire circle so everyone receives the support of the whole—and often learns much about themselves in the process.

You might be surprised by the emotional release this can generate. Once this activity is in full swing it stirs an empathy in the group that allows members to "pick up" on what another member most needs to hear. To site a personal example, when I did this activity with a small group one woman there struck me as an Earth mother. When I said this, tears began to fall from her eyes. Apparently she'd been struggling with a decision about whether or not to move to the country and start an herb farm. This well-timed observation gave her the confidence necessary to do just that. When you take the time to create a group that is aware and alert, you can literally begin transforming people's lives and help them pursue their dreams.

ACTIVITY: Refreshing the Ties That Bind

After being together for awhile, any group can find it gets lazy about the way it moves through observance. A certain depth gets lost, small arguments may erupt, and sharing may become superficial. This is perfectly natural. Keeping two people finely attuned to one another and enthusiastic about a relationship is difficult enough, let alone 10 or 20! With this tendency in mind, I recommend that groups periodically stop and enact a ritual where everyone recognizes and signifies his or her desire to refresh the group's intimate connections. In turn, once revitalized, the magick of that group will show signs of improvement by moving away from rote liturgy into inspired, fulfilling rites.

To begin, decorate the altar or center of the room with one candle for each person in the group and a larger candle that represents the group as a unit. You also need one long piece of string or yarn per person. (Have each person choose a suitable color to personalize this activity.) One end of all these strands should be knotted onto a ring or piece of wood.

The creation of sacred space is more a matter of attitude than anything else. If you approach an area as special and respect-worthy, it can be sacred. Many religious traditions add something to this attitude, such as prayer, invocations, and ritualistic tools, to create a unique ambiance that is honored as holy.

After the sacred space is prepared, each person in turn steps up to the string bundle and picks up his or her strand. As he or she does, he or she tells everyone about a hope or wish he or she has for the group's progress. He or she then knots that energy into the whole bundle. This continues until everyone takes a turn. The strand of knots gets left on the altar to be given into the keeping of a priest/ess, who will bring it to any gathering where the themes of unity, communication, and harmony are being stressed.

Next, each person will take up his or her individual candle and touch the flame to that of the central candle. Together the group should chant something, such as:

"UNITY AND TRUST, A MAGICKAL MUST.

BY THE LIGHT OF THE FLAME,

HARMONY WE CLAIM!"

Allow the energy in this chant to naturally rise to a pinnacle and then fall into silence. Each person blows out his or her individual candle and puts it back on the table. At this point proceed with a time of fellowship to discuss how the ritual felt, whether something seemed to come alive during the process, and what people might have learned about each other's goals.

Coming out of the Broom Closet

One circumstance when our communication skills as Witches are tested is when we're discussing the Craft with people outside magickal traditions. This is very different from working one-on-one or with a magickal group. The reactions you can anticipate receiving run the full emotional gamut from fear to joyful acceptance.

This makes our job pretty tough, and it requires that we know intimately of what we speak so we can answer difficult questions. It also requires a certain diplomacy on our part. One does not simply declare their witchiness over a side dish of carrots at the dining room table! The decision to make others aware of our Witchcraft is very personal, and should be thought out thoroughly in advance.

The best first step is trying to find a common ground upon which to build. Leave a few nonthreatening magickal books lying around for folks to see and wonder about. Metaphysical dream interpretation and herbalism are two good examples of subject matter that is considered "safe." Alternatively, toss in a movie about the Craft, such as *Practical Magic*, and leave it playing. See if the movie inspires any questions. Bear in mind, however, that you have many negative stereotypes to overcome. Be patient with people. It took years for my family to totally understand my path, but now they support it fully.

When you decide to enter into discussions with people about the Craft, there are some other good rules to follow that I've found very helpful especially for public speaking.

- ◆ **Research.** Plain and simple, know your history, know where magickal traditions come from, and know how they've changed. Be able to explain things such as why animal sacrifice was once very popular but is no longer acceptable.

- ◆ **Emphasize Wicca as a religion.** Wicca is recognized by the U.S. military as a religion, and the chaplains of all armed forces have information about what constitutes our faith in their handbook. Really, Wicca is no different than any other belief system in that it encourages us to honor the Sacred and be the best people we can.

♦ **Keep calm.** Never lose your cool or it will bite you on the butt later.

♦ **Even if a question seems silly to you, answer it with sincerity.** Bear in mind that you may be the first real Witch this person has ever met.

♦ **Be tolerant.** Don't fall into "I'm right, you're wrong" speech patterns. Tolerance builds understanding.

♦ **Don't be apologetic.** Being a Witch isn't something to be ashamed of. It's a proud title with a legitimate history of helping individuals and whole communities. More importantly, it's your way of life!

♦ **Provide small consumable bits of information at a time.** Giving too much, too soon only confuses things. Make one point well and you've done a good job. Build on that foundation later after they've had time to digest the initial information.

♦ **Know when to speak and when to listen.** Let people have their say, but also know when someone is running away with the show. Similarly, try to recognize when someone is simply goading you, and not really wanting honest answers.

♦ **Avoid cosmic lingo.** A lot of words in magickal traditions are misunderstood by the public, so if you can find viable alternatives, do so.

♦ **Look responsible.** Appearances mean a lot.

♦ **Be on time.** If you're speaking for any public function, Pagan Standard Time has no place. Witches and Pagans both have gotten a bad reputation for being unprofessional in this area. Remember, being prompt means you respect and value *other* people's time!

Overall, following these guidelines leads to much more successful Craft-related discussions. But again I caution against expecting huge changes quickly. We have a lot of re-educating to do in our homes, our offices, our schools, the political arena, and so forth. If you can help one person at a time overcome past portraits of the Craft, you're doing great. Keep it up so that all Witches can open their broom closets freely in today's world.

Word Power for Magick

Language has an amazing effect on the way our magick manifests. Consider the power in this simple phrase: "I can." How does saying it change the energy in and around you? How does thinking it change the way you act?

Or what about the language of prayer? Here, a voice rises in supplication and honestly trusts an answer will come. Throughout the room, to the four winds, and from there to the world, this wish is communicated, changing the energy along the entire network of life! Chanting, affirmations, mantras, and the like work similarly.

The potential of harmonic language to augment our magickal methods for healing, awareness, concentration, peace, and communication is nearly unlimited. It can also change our outlooks about words such as *Witch*. But how do we put these ideas to use? I propose creating a key word list that you can keep in your Book of Shadows. This list would be composed of terms and phrases that you strongly associate with a specific type of energy, perspective, or manifestation. For example:

- ♦ **Creativity:** flow, mastery, vision, imagination.
- ♦ **Strength:** endurance, persistence, tenacity.
- ♦ **Joy:** contentment, satisfaction, fulfillment.
- ♦ **Magick:** intuition, symmetrical, focus, Witch.
- ♦ **Prosperity:** abundance, security, providence.

You can use your finished list for many witchy activities. If you needed to overcome a creative blockage, you might whisper the word "flow" to yourself repeatedly before going to sleep. Or you could use key words as part of incantations and invocations aimed at those goals. Design affirmations and chants with the words, or charge objects (such as amulets) with specific phrases.

What's nice here is that in creating highly personal spells and rituals, you've effectively applied terms with which you have a strong emotional connection. Better still, your voice is something you have with you wherever you go, so the magick is portable—no matter where we travel, we can think and speak our spiritual goals and begin manifesting that magick in today's world.

Chapter 3

As Within, So Without

Peace is the evening star of the soul.
—*Caleb Colton*

C hapters 1 and 2 were designed to inspire the process of internal change, and then to begin manifesting and expressing those changes effectively with the people in and around our lives. The next step comes in re-creating our environment. A spiritually healthy living space is a key ingredient for successful, empowered modern Witches. After all, it's really hard to focus on magickal ideas when our home lives are upside down, and everything around us speaks of mundane matters.

With this in mind, it stands to reason that we should begin to alter the areas in which we spend significant amounts of time so they better represent who we are and where we are going as spiritual beings. While each person has limits as to how explicit this expression becomes, even small touches can mean a lot. There's no need to hang a signpost on your house saying "Witch within" or to decorate your other haunts with bundles of brooms to indicate your religious preference. If you *want* to, that's a whole other matter!

I'm in a situation where I have friends and family who aren't always overly comfortable with "the magick thing." When these people visit, I want them to feel welcome. The question then becomes one of making personally meaningful changes in my environment without scaring the pants off old Aunt Belle or making Uncle Dom antsy.

Because Witches often have to confine their magick to indoor settings (not everyone has a yard these days), this chapter goes both inside and outside the home, office, and other frequented hangouts to discuss ways to make spiritually pleasing alterations. This way, no matter your environment, you can decide among a variety of ways to transform that space from one that's ordinary into something more witchy, keeping wisdom as an ally.

Home Sweet Home

Be it a house, apartment, boarding house, or whatever, our home is our spiritual castle. This is where you spend the greatest amount of your time, and also the area where you can be your witchy self, usually without worries. If you happen to be in a household with others who are uncomfortable with magick, you'll have to tweak some of the suggestions here a bit so as to remain sensitive to the people who share your roof. If, however, you live alone or with people who respect your path, the ways in which you can express this path in your environment are really only limited by your imagination.

Because New Age has become fashionable, we have a wide variety of art available to decorate our personal spaces. Better still, people see crystals, dragons, and all manner of other trinkets every day at the mall, so few visitors will think twice about your choice of embellishments! A Witch who practices a shamanic form of the Craft, for example, strategically places forest scenes or carvings of animals around the house. Someone drawn to the Dianic tradition of the Craft might choose sculptures of the various classical goddesses and books on women in history.

ACTIVITY: Accenting the Elements

For this activity you'll need to know which part of your living space faces North so you can determine the rest of the cardinal directions. You'll also need four decorative items, one each for the four Elements of Earth, Air, Fire, and Water (corresponding to North, East, South, and West, respectively).

The options from which to choose your tokens are virtually endless. Need some ideas? For Air, how about yellow-white flower arrangements, an air conditioner, wind chimes, paper airplanes, or a feather duster? For Fire, a candle is perfect, as is a fireplace, stove, heating vent, oil lamps, or a potted cactus. Moving to Water, we might consider a humidifier, hot tub, hose, sink, seashell, model boats, floating candles, fish bowls, or even fire extinguishers. Finally, for Earth, a growing plant, a change jar, a picture of your favorite pet/animal, wooden carvings, or herb bundles all suit.

Once you gather your tokens together, take a moment to charge and bless them for their purpose. Perhaps hold your hands down over the items, visualizing pure white light pouring into each, while saying:

"OF EARTH AND SKY, FIRE AND FOAM,

ALL AROUND BLESS MY HOME!"

Take the token and put it as close as possible to the cardinal point to which it corresponds. You now have four reminders of the Elements of magick in place, which can also be used in establishing sacred space any time you wish.

Lighting, Color, and Music

Lighting, color, and music can improve the psychic-spiritual energies around us. We know, for example, that natural light is healthy and often lifts depression. Colors also influence our moods and energy levels. Music, of course, is the universal language through which we can convey vibrations throughout rooms, a whole house, and sometimes even further.

In choosing light, color, and sounds for our magickal living space, we need to keep in mind the function of each area, our personal needs/goals, and, of course, personal taste. For example, while bright blue might be great for inspiring hope in some people, if you don't like that color, it probably won't create the desired effect. Some basic correspondences are provided in the chart on page 57 for your consideration; you should tweak this list so it's more reflective of your vision before applying it.

ACTIVITY: Applying Colors and Sounds

For this activity, consider one thing that you want to cultivate into your life. For sake of example, let's say it's patience. Review the list on page 57 to see which colors and sounds reflect that virtue. In this case it's sky blue and New Age music. If you agree with this correspondence, you might then start wearing more light blue articles of clothing, burning pale blue candles in your spells, spending more time beneath the clear blue sky, adding some blue-toned light bulbs to your living space, or putting up sheer blue curtains to disperse the color's vibration throughout a room. Alternatively, perhaps you'd prefer to work with white, focusing your attention on a simple white wall while listening to the sounds of a Tibetan prayer bowl to calm your spirit.

In an inspired moment, a friend of mine tossed some glitter into his ceiling paint so that at night, with a candle burning and some quiet music playing in the background, the visual impression is that of lying beneath a clear night's sky. The effect for

Color	Correspondences	Sounds
crystal white	sincerity; purity; protection; centering; divinity; healing; transformation	singular sounds, such as a gong or bell, for focus
bright red	vibrant energy; Fire; inspiration; sexuality; emotions; vitality; healing; purification	intense dynamic music; drumming; heartbeat; crackling fire
fiery orange	stimulation; will; Fall; abstracts; theory; intuition; spirit	passionate music; birds after a storm; sounds of dawn and dusk
golden yellow	attraction; charm; Summer fruitfulness; confidence; solar magick; trust; strength	rock and roll; bright, clear sounds; children laughing and playing
pastel yellow	Air; Spring; beginnings; psychism; creativity; rebirth; goals	oldies; upbeat instrumental music
forest green	growth; sustenance; fertility; Earth magick; nature; the body; material needs	classical music; wilderness sounds; deep-toned drums and bells
ivy green	feelings; belief; connections; coping; healing	hushed music; silence
midnight blue	Water magick; Wiccan studies; dreams; wishes	the Blues; crickets; New Age or celestial music
sky blue	peace; understanding; hopefulness; patience	New Age music; Spring sounds; wind chimes; church bells
violet	spirit; power; love; honor; wisdom; enchantment; the mysteries; fairies	impassioned opera; owls; magickal music (for example, chants)

meditation and other magickal processes is really neat! It's as if the entire room gets transported outside and the universe lays at your feet.

Not everyone trying this exercise is going to start repainting his or her home, but this gives you some good food for thought. Encompass your life with beauty and magick and in the process you cannot help but empower the Witch within.

Magick Room by Room

Have you ever thought about using different areas of your house for different types of magick? This is a great way to fill every corner of your reality with good vibrations while also adding some meaning to your spells and rituals. For example, cooking magick works best in the kitchen or pantry. The bedroom might be a good location for spells pertaining to health, stress relief, rest, passion, and dream weaving. Here are some other correspondences to consider:

- ◆ **Bathroom:** privacy spells, cleansing, purification, self-images.
- ◆ **Bedroom:** fertility, romance, intimacy.
- ◆ **Dining room:** kinship, unity, hospitality, fellowship.
- ◆ **Study/Studio:** learning, knowledge, business.
- ◆ **Family room:** strengthening bonds, harmony.
- ◆ **Cellar:** grounding, Earth magick, building foundations.
- ◆ **Sun room:** solar magick (or wind magick if the windows are open), energy, emotional warmth.

ACTIVITY: Kitchen Magick 101

To give yourself a hands-on example of how to put room magick to work effectively, try this bit of pantry wizardry the next time you have a witchy friend coming to visit. Begin with some frozen bread dough. Let this defrost and rise properly, then blend in a little dill and a hint of dry onion to promote a strong, stable relationship with your visitor. As you knead the herbs into the bread (perhaps in the dining room for kinship, or in the kitchen, which is the heart of the home), keep a strong sense of purpose in your mind, and channel that purpose into the kneading process. Baking warms the magick to perfection, then you can serve the bread in a suitable room, where slicing releases the energy and eating internalizes it. Any type of magick can be worked in any room, and the more one makes magick, the more positive energy is left behind.

I recommend trying to do some type of magickal activity in every room of your house on a regular basis. This will charge the wood and plaster with your energy. Like a giant battery, each room will absorb that positive power so that you are always surrounded with the essence of magick.

ACTIVITY: Banishing Unwanted Energies

Witches are barraged with negativity every day from many different places. And just as dust accumulates on furniture, the residual negativity you collect can begin affecting the sacred space of your home, not to mention your attitude. To help keep that from happening, you can perform this spell to safeguard your home from unwanted energies.

For the spell, you'll need a large bowl of salt water. I suggest performing this spell four times a year on the four Quarter dates (March 22, June 22, September 22, and December 22) to continually support the protection you're creating. Take the salt water to every window, doorway, or opening throughout the house (don't forget electrical outlets). Dab it on each spot and say:

"BONDS OF POWER, BONDS OF LIGHT,

GROW STRONG, PROTECT, DEFEND.

LET ALL DARKNESS TAKE TO FLIGHT!"

Speak firmly and confidently, keeping the image of a firmly locked door in your mind with anything you don't want around left outside.

If you want, you can combine this activity with a good sage smudging to banish and purify anything that's lingering around to literally clear the air on all levels. Alternatively, make small herb bundles (basil, dill, and marjoram for protection, blessing, and love, respectively) and place them strategically around the house. The aromatic effect continues to release magick into your home until the bundles lose their scent (in about six months).

ACTIVITY: Welcoming New Housemates

My friends and family often joke that we have a revolving door here and seem to always have someone staying with us for extended times. When this happens, that person becomes a temporary family member, which shifts the entire dynamic of the sacred house and magickal family. Other circumstances that create this shift include the birth of a child and getting a new pet. In all cases, you have to re-tune yourself and your home to make the associated transition easier and maintain overall harmony.

For this activity, each person in your home should pick out a symbolic token to present to the new housemate. The token should somehow represent that individual's role as a part of the greater whole and make him or her feel welcome. For example, for a new pet, one might get a pet ID tag with the family's phone number engraved. For long-term guests, you might present a coffee mug or a set of towels.

When everyone is ready, gather in a circle with the new house member in the middle. Each person in turn should present his or her token, explain its significance, and perhaps exchange a warm hug. With people, this part of the activity is very important. It often provides insights that will be useful in living with them responsibly and in an atmosphere of trust.

ACTIVITY: Cleansing and Reclaiming Your Space

Because our society is mobile and roommates are common, it brings to bear the question of what happens when someone moves out, or when a particularly dominant guest leaves. Once again you're coping with an energy shift, and the living space might seem odd and imbalanced. You might actually feel like a stranger to your own space because you had to drastically rearrange it to make temporary space for that individual!

This is a good time to cleanse the space again. (I like to wash the floors with lemon water). After the cleansing, it's time to reclaim your territory. Move the furniture, paint something, polish, smudge, adorn, and launder. Do whatever it takes to make the space feel emotionally and magickally satisfying.

When this work is completed, take some time just for you. Break out some favorite tea or wine, light a candle, put on your favorite New Age tunes, and look at your handiwork. The effort of cleaning and rearranging has enough physical energy in it to redirect the patterns of your entire home into a fresh, witchy motif that's wholly you!

◆ ◆ ◆

For Witches in an urban setting, activities such as the ones recommended in this section are vitally important to your spiritual state of mind. The concrete jungle isn't overly kind to magickal energy, often tainting, draining, or depleting it altogether. By regularly maintaining your home, you'll keep it as a spiritually safe haven in which your Witchery can grow and be nourished to perfection.

At Work

The average person spends between 20 and 40 hours a week in a work-related environment. You're expected to maintain a certain demeanor, perform tasks consistently, and be courteous even when you want to scream. For many Witches, going to work also often means tucking their magickal selves in their pocket where they can't be seen behind the mundane veneer.

I know for me this last part was very hard to manage because it felt hypocritical—especially when those conversations about holiday celebrations, religion, and similar discussions come up. I found myself biting my tongue for fear of misunderstanding or, worse yet, losing my job. I'm sure some of you face (or have faced) similar situations. Since we spend approximately 20 percent of our personal time in this difficult predicament, we need to consider ways of improving the climate so it has a stronger metaphysical focus without being overly conspicuous.

Decorations

An easy way to subtly change the aura throughout your work area is via small embellishments. Live plants (the Earth element), crystals (energy), cards from friends (positive reinforcement), family photos (support), and similar items can refresh the spark of magick in at least one spot. If your work environment isn't one where you have a private office, cubicle, or desk, such as a factory or a hospital, these items will likely have to be restricted to a locker, but then opening the door to that locker also opens the magick you placed carefully within!

When I worked as a secretary I had a shelf above my computer where I kept objects to represent the Elements: a seashell (Water), a pine cone (Earth), some potpourri (Air), and a white candle (Fire). Before I brought these to the office, I blessed and energized them. I also took them home for regular cleansings and recharging. Looking at the final effect, no one really thought anything of it. It appeared like normal bric-a-brac, but to me they were much more than that. They were symbols of my Witchery, of the Elements, and all I hold dear.

Charging Your Decorations

Charge each token you plan to take to your workspace in sunlight, moonlight, or any other way suited to your path. (Sunlight accents the conscious, logical mind and aids with strength, leadership, clarity, and connecting with the God aspect. Moonlight accents the subconscious, intuitive mind and helps with nurturing, healing, creativity, and connecting with the Goddess aspect.) Have a firm idea in mind of what you want this object to represent in that setting (if you can visualize where the item will physically be, all the better)—be it a special cup that symbolizes the Goddess, a crystal charged-up for concentration, or whatever—and keep that goal in mind while you energize and bless it. Then, when you get a private moment at work, place the objects out using a whispered incantation so that the magick you stored within goes into active mode.

Protection

Protective magick is a gift you give yourself at work. Even when you really love your job, most people find working stimulates a certain amount of stress and pressure that can adversely affect magickal pursuits at the end of the day. By bringing a little safe energy into the working world, you can often shake off a lot of those bad vibes.

Protective Amulets

Sachets are the easiest form of amulet. All you do is take a scrap of fabric and common household herbs, and tie the fabric around the herbs. Some good choices for carrying with you to work include apple peel for peace, dill for mental clarity, bay for protection, chamomile for success and calmness, and cloves to hinder gossip. Your sachet can be kept inconspicuously in a purse, desk drawer, or filing cabinet. If you don't have any of these components, try simple salt instead. This has been used throughout world history as a cleanser and protector. And, if you feel particularly in need of safety just take out a pinch of the herbs or salt and toss it in the general direction from which the trouble seems to emanate. Just remember to refill your sachet later.

Blending In

On those days when you feel overexposed, this activity often produces results within three days. With practice you'll be able to do this anytime, anywhere when you just want to retreat a bit from the forefront.

To begin, consider the chameleon. For those of you practicing a shamanic form of Wicca, go to the middle realm of the world tree and seek this creature's spirit for instruction in the art of camouflage. For the rest of us, studying the creature at a zoo, in a book, or on a Web site will help the effect of this exercise.

Next, see yourself in your mind's eye in the setting where the problem exists. Note every detail around you, especially how you're juxtaposed against the backdrop. Now, slowly let the edges of your body get fuzzy and blurry. See the color of your skin and hair shifting to mirror the background that surrounds, just like a chameleon blends into its surroundings. Continue until there is no sign of self in the portrait but for an odd displacement where you were. Do this visualization every day for three days before going into the situation where you feel overexposed.

Basically you're hiding your energy from direct viewing. The only people who might not be affected are those with natural psychic skills or high levels of empathy. And, by the way, this exercise is a very good one for those wishing to improve their glamoury skills where specific shifts in the aura are desired. (Glamoury is an auric shift that changes self-perception as well as others' perception of you.) Simply change the activity to see the texture or color of your aura and body altering to mirror what you wish to communicate to others nonverbally.

ACTIVITY: Binding Problematic Co-workers

I have yet to meet someone who gets along with everyone where they work—unless he or she works alone! If you're experiencing problems with a particular person, this old folk spell will help. Everyone who tries it has reported some level of success. Either the person tones down hostilities, transfers, or sometimes leaves the company altogether!

You'll need a piece of that person's stationery or a scrap of paper from his or her desk. Write the person's name on the paper and fold it inward three times. Wrap the paper with white and red string then put it in an ice cube tray covered in water. Freeze this to slow down or "freeze" any unwarranted bad intentions on his or her part. The idea is to put a protective barrier between you and them (the ice) so their negativity reflects right back to them. Again, if the person does nothing untoward, this spell is totally harmless!

On the Road

At the turn of the 20th century, going a few miles was a huge jaunt. Today we travel thousands of miles without a second thought. This represents a huge change in our society, one that presents more than a few problems for Witches. For example, a Witch who prefers to use an athame for magick often has trouble carrying this tool on airplanes, and certain ritual wines may not be allowed by authorities due to food and drug laws. With such constraints in mind, I began to consider how we could adapt and transform our modes of transportation so that they're filled with magick and vision. The ideas and activities here are a result of that personal exploration.

Safe Travel

Every day we turn on the news and hear of automobile accidents or airplane crashes, which certainly inspires me to look into protective magickal methods before I venture very far! In designing your spells for safe travel, some imagery of the vehicle itself is a powerful component. This gives you a place to focus your energy very specific to the goal at hand. I know we can't go around blessing our airplanes directly, but there's nothing that says you can't bless a paper airplane with the name of the airline and flight number on it!

You could also make a travel charm out of a paper or cloth bag filled with bay, chamomile, dandelion, lemon, and pine. These ingredients promote protection, success, wish fulfillment, joy, and safety, respectively. On the outside of this bundle put the rune of protection (this looks like a Y that has the middle portion extended upward). In the car, keep this in your glove compartment. On a bus, plane, or train, keep it in your briefcase, purse, or carry-on luggage.

Travel Chants

In those moments when you haven't had the chance to create a protective charm, there's nothing that says you can't chant. Aloud or to yourself, words have tremendous power to change the energy around you and get it moving in a more productive way. Here are some examples to try or adapt for yourself:

Stuck Subway:

"BENEATH THE GROUND, LET MAGICK ABOUND.

GOD/DESS HEAR MY PLEA,

LET THIS TRAIN MOVE FREE!"

Traffic Jam:

"LADY AND LORD, I NOW BEHOOVE,

MAKE THIS TRAFFIC START TO MOVE!

Plane Turbulence:

GOD/DESS NO MATTER WHERE I ROAM,

TAKE ME SAFELY BACK TO HOME!"

Bicycle and Bus Blessings:

"THE WHEELS TURN ROUND, MAGICK ABOUNDS.

SAFETY TO ME, SO MOTE IT BE!"

True, these poems aren't great works of literary art, but they're easy to remember. Keep repeating them to yourself in your mind until you feel calmer or the situation changes, or both!

Potent Portables

Protection and safety certainly aren't the only kinds of energy we would like to keep with us on the road. Specifically, there are items we carry all the time that can become amulets, charms, and talismans.

Wallet, Purse, or Pocket

Dab some patchouli oil on your wallet or purse to make it into a prosperity charm. Put a coin with the year of your birth on it inside or in your pocket for ongoing luck. Carry aromatic sachets or incense matches of a suitable scent so they accent your goals for that day. Keep some personal perfume handy and use it to mark your territory no matter where you may be.

Clothes

What we wear makes a difference in how we feel and behave. If you don't believe me, put on jeans and a comfortable T-shirt for an hour, switch into formal clothes for an hour, and note the shift in your demeanor. When you put on clothing, you symbolically accept the energy it represents, and this energy certainly goes with you everywhere! So, why not blend in a little Witchery for good measure?

Try washing your clothes in an herbal tincture to energize them for whatever task lies ahead (such as orange for love or health). Alternatively, place a bundle of herbs in the dryer where the heat will activate your energy. When you travel, take something special that makes you feel witchy and is warm to change into. You could also add pieces of clothing into your wardrobe whose colors augment the magick on which you've been working (such as red for strength or blue for peace).

Jewelry

Many people wear earrings these days—not to mention any number of other trinkets. The only difference between what they wear and what you do will be intention. Witches know that thoughtful adornment can create just the right transitions in our aura to help achieve our goals. For example, I have a friend who wears star and moon jewelry because she's an astronomer. She blesses her jewelry to give her greater awareness of her work, but to everyone around her, the jewelry just looks like neat bobbles!

Look through the items you already own and see if any have specific meaning to you. If so, cleanse, bless, and empower each item so it resonates with that meaning each time you wear it. You can cleanse items in a variety of ways, including sprinkling them with salt or lemon water, moving them through incense (such as frankincense or sage), or even visualizing the item being filled to overflowing with white light so any residual negativity has no place to hide. Blessing often means taking the item before your vision of the Divine, holding it up (or placing your palms down over it), and praying for divine sanctification on that tool for its given function in your sacred space.

For example, I have a labradorite necklace that I wear for spiritual teaching. This is the incantation I used to energize it:

"Spirit in this stone of blue,

let my words ring of truth.

Honesty, kindness, a loving heart,

when I don this the magick impart!"

One word of caution here about portable magick. Don't get overly analytical about what constitutes a suitable charm. If it feels right, use it. I once kept an Inspector Gadget doll in my purse because my son insisted I carry it. For me it represented love and resourcefulness. Similarly, a scrap from your childhood blanket, a theater ticket, bits of ribbon, and similar items are easily transportable and often deeply meaningful. The positive emotional response they engender is what makes the magick!

♦ ♦ ♦

By scanning this chapter it's pretty easy to see how almost every experience and object in our everyday world has the potential for magick if we meet the moment with a fresh, expectant eye. From protecting and cleansing your home to carrying the magick with you, your witchy nature is slowly filling your reality to overflowing. From inside your living space to the great outdoors and beyond, you really have the power to transform every moment of living into a special, magickal memory.

Chapter 4

Granny Green Witch

The Earth has music for those who listen.
—Shakespeare

G ranny Green Witch is a nickname I've obtained because I love puttering with the Earth and working with herbs. I'm aware that many Witches don't have a lot of time for gardening or crafts, but for those who do I think it offers a tremendous balance to the concrete jungle. Even small bits of time working with the Mother and her treasures brings us back in touch with the amazing spirit of our planet, not to mention all the lessons it provides.

Magickal Ecology

A wise Witch recognizes that the Earth is a valuable resource that needs our respect and protection. Yes, this means very mundane things, such as recycling, using nature's storehouse wisely, and picking up garbage. On a spiritual level, however, even more needs to be done.

The Earth has been wounded, so its auric energy (manifested somewhat in the atmosphere) is also out of balance. The most notable example of this is the ozone layer, which is gaping open like an untended sore. The good news is that we can use concrete efforts combined with our magick to generate positive energy aimed at helping the Earth's healing process along (and heightening public awareness at the same time).

One such effort is composting. It is a great way to enrich the soil, but, depending on your location, it may require getting a special container. Some of the items you can compost include lime, bones or bone dust, coffee, fish, animal manure, grass, seaweed, peanut shells, herb and vegetable ends, hardwood, coal ash, meat scraps, egg shells, leaves, sawdust, hair, fruit, oak bark, and leather. Once your blend is properly decomposed and ready to add to the soil, mix in the following herbs, which deter pests: nettle, dandelion, yarrow, chamomile, and valerian. Stir the mix clockwise to draw in positive energy, saying:

"BLESSINGS AND HEALTH,

RESTORE THE EARTH'S WEALTH!"

You can then use this in window-boxes or your magickal garden, or you can take it to a forest or other natural region to bless the land.

Here are a few activities to help you improve your relationship with Earth.

Activity: Megalith Magick

Many Witches, Neo-Pagans, and New Age practitioners believe that the ancients were very aware of the Earth's magnetic fields when they built ancient structures, including megaliths. These structures seem to connect to or augment the Earth's ley lines so that the Earth's energy flows freely where it needs to go. Unfortunately, as a result of construction, war, and pollution, many of these natural lines of force have been broken or erased. The idea behind this activity is to create a small megalith aimed at rebuilding a ley line or blessing an area of land.

Find a suitable spot. Remember your megalith need not be huge to be effective. You can try dousing (water Witchery using a Y-shaped branch) as one means of discovering energy lines, or simply opening your senses to the Earth's music and letting her guide you to a place.

After you discover a region where you'd like to place some stones, next consider the type of stones. Do you simply want to sprinkle charged crystals into the Earth? Set up a circle of stones? Make some other magickal pattern? It's up to you; do what feels right. No matter what your choice, however, keep a strong image of your goal in mind all the while you design and work.

I strongly suggest returning to this spot regularly to cast spells, hold rituals, meditate, or whatever. This way you can direct your witchy energy along the power lines created there to bless others and the Earth, and to support your magickal goals.

Activity: Healing Visualization

Go to a natural location where you can sit on the ground. If this isn't possible, sit on a floor of your home that's close to soil (the cellar is a good location). If you want, you can bring some brown or green candles as a focus, as they represent Earth's tones.

Put your hands down next to you. Breathe deeply and turn your attention to the pulse and rhythm of the Earth below. Feel it breathe with the wind; hear the heartbeat in surges of water. Once you feel attuned to this ebb and flow, begin seeing a white-green light pouring down from above into your hands and out to the Earth. Envision that light slowly spreading out from you in all directions, holding the Earth in a warm, healthy hug.

At this point you might want to begin chanting something such as:

"EARTH BE ONE. EARTH BE HEALED.

BY THIS SPELL YOUR STRENGTH IS SEALED."

If you feel creative, add other verses directed at specific parts of the environment, such as water, animals, and trees. Let this chant naturally reach a pinnacle by which time the visualization should have wrapped the whole Earth in glowing wholeness.

When you're done, take a nice long walk to refresh yourself and enjoy the planet's wonders.

Activity: A Plant Called Earth

For this activity you need a potted plant or tree that you can tend regularly. It should be one that seems to need a little TLC. Name your chosen plant "Earth." For the next year, give this plant as much physical and spiritual pampering as possible. Put charged crystals around it, pray over it, and channel healing energy into your mini-Earth. By the end of that year I'm willing to bet you'll find your plant flourishing, and your appreciation for nature growing too. Indirectly this helps the whole network of life. Remember: A symbol is no less potent than what it represents in magick.

Activity: An Earth Pledge

Once a year, or at an interval of your choosing, a green-minded Witch may wish to make a pledge to the Earth to continue to tend it with loving hands. Here is one example you can consider and adapt to reflect your personal goals for how you wish to help the Earth in today's world:

I PLEDGE TO GREET EACH DAY AS A NEW BEGINNING,

TO WALK WITH GENTLE, RESPECTFUL STEPS ON THIS EARTH,

TO LIVE IN PEACEFUL RECIPROCITY WITH NATURE,

TO SEE THE BEST IN MY FELLOW CREATURES.

I PLEDGE TO GIVE SOME TIME EACH WEEK TO RECLAIMING THE
    LAND,
TO RENEW PLANTS AND ANIMALS THAT HUMANKIND, MISUSED
TO LEARN THE OLD WAYS, CLOSE TO THE SOIL,
TO HEAL, TO NURTURE, TO GROW IN ONENESS WITH GAIA.
I PLEDGE TO LIVE A MAGICKAL LIFE EACH DAY, EACH MOMENT
    AND TRY TO MEET NEEDS SPONTANEOUSLY,
TO SERVE WITH LOVING HANDS AND HEART,
TO WORK IN PERFECT TRUST.
SO MOTE IT BE.

Do not enter into such a pledge just because I say so! This represents a serious commitment you're making to yourself, the earth, and the Sacred. It should be one made only after serious contemplation.

◆ ◆ ◆

Don't forget to use good common sense when conducting metaphysical activities such as the ones in this chapter. Buy from producers who use animal- and Earth-friendly processes. Support reputable ecological groups. Make efforts in and around your neighborhood to inspire events such as paper drives and tree plantings. And, in your own home, try to find a way to reuse what you can and replace only what you cannot. True wholeness for this planet cannot happen if we ignore its body while tending its spirit.

Witch Gardens

One of the easiest ways to get back down to Earth is through gardening. Be it a window-box or full-fledged outdoor effort, working with the soil often feeds the human soul. It also makes us more intimately aware of life's web so that as we weave our spells, we can honor that network.

There are a lot of choices for magickal gardens, but starting small may be the best idea. Gardens take time, and so many of us are time-challenged these days that adding another project might prove more burdensome than spiritual. By keeping the effort small, you avoid this pitfall. Look to doing an arrangement on your window sill or something similar at first. If you find you want to expand later, you certainly can! Here are some ideas to consider in planning your magickal garden.

Magickal Herbs

Herbs are among the easiest things to grow indoors, and they're certainly among today's Witch's most useful components for spells and rituals. To plan this garden, make a list of the herbs you use regularly in spellcraft. Compare this list to seed requirements for depth of soil, sunlight, and so forth, so you can determine which ones are easiest for you to grow at home. Then just get your seeds, bless your soil, and watch your magick grow! When the herbs are fully grown, blend fresh-picked magick into any meal or methodology simply by harvesting what you need. Remember to thank the plant for its gift. Note, too, that this particular garden benefits tremendously from the crystal magick method (provided later in the chapter).

Zodiac Garden

A person born under a particular sign might want to create a small garden filled with plants governed by that sign. Why? Because then they have highly attuned components that mingle with personal, celestial vibrations harmoniously. For example, if you're a Libra you might want to grow yarrow or primroses, while a Virgo might grow lavender or valerian. To augment the energy of this garden, put tiny tumbled crystals in the soil that are also attuned to the specific Zodiac sign (lapis or turquoise for Libra, agate for Virgo).

Meditative Space

More suited to an outdoor setting or a home where you can have planters in several windows of one room, meditative gardens are just that: gardens created to enhance our state of awareness for meditation. So you might choose sunflower and/or sage for wisdom, roses and/or thyme for psychic awareness, violet and/or lavender for inner harmony, and so on The key here is to pick the plants for your garden so they're suited to both the energies you want and your available space. To improve the energy further, add small pieces of sodalite to the bottom of the planting area, as these provide natural drainage and bear the energy of meditative focus.

Elemental Garden

For this garden you'll need a large round planter that you can quarter off; the idea is to have one section for each Element/direction. Since every plant on the Earth has been categorized for it's Elemental association, finding ones you like to use for magick to plant in the right Quarter shouldn't be hard. Here are a few ideas:

- ♦ **East/Air:** beans, clover, dandelion, lavender, sage.
- ♦ **South/Fire:** basil, celery, dill, onion, radish, rosemary.
- ♦ **West/Water:** catnip, cucumber, daisy, morning glory, rose.
- ♦ **North/Earth:** alfalfa, peas, primrose, tulip, vetivert.

Inside the home this particular arrangement provides a living, growing Wheel and Sacred Circle that blesses everything and everyone within. Outdoors, Elemental gardens can be made large enough so as to have walkways in them where you can commune with the Elements, pray, or whatever. Better still, the next time you need some fresh Elemental energy for a spell or ritual, you need only pick a small snippet for that occasion!

Enhancing Your Garden

Once you know what type of garden you plan to design, the next step is adding even more magickal symbolism to the process. Here are three suggestions for doing just that.

Gardening by the Moon

Up until 100 years ago you could readily find farmers looking to the moon for signs indicating when best to plant, weed, and harvest. Truth be known, if you look closely, you'll find a lot of Witches still doing that! But to apply this idea, you'll need this list of lunar cycles and how they affect plants:

- **Waxing moon:** Plant above-ground vegetation, such as celery, asparagus, cabbage, herbs, and flowering plants.

- **Full moon:** Good for peppers, pumpkins, tomatoes, melon flowering vines, and garlic.

- **Waning moon:** Plant peas or underground vegetation, such as carrots, potatoes, radishes, bulb flowers.

- **Dark moon:** Best time to weed and turn the soil.

Alternatively, if you feel like getting more detailed than this list allows, you can look to each moonsign (check a good astrological calendar) for assistance in your green witchery as follows:

- **Moon in Aries:** Plant only garlic and onions.

- **Moon in Taurus:** Root crops, such as potatoes; also leafy vegetables.

- **Moon in Gemini:** Weed and cultivate. Planting is not recommended.

- **Moon in Cancer:** Graft, transplant, sow, and improved rewards.

- **Moon in Leo:** Use your insect-banishing formula now (see the activity on page 80).

- **Moon in Libra:** Flowers, root crops, vines, lettuce, corn, and vine-producing plants.

- ◆ **Moon in Scorpio:** Excellent time for any type of planting. Augment this energy with the crystal technique in the Crystal Gardening section.
- ◆ **Moon in Sagittarius:** Productive for plants that like dryness.
- ◆ **Moon in Capricorn:** Tubers and root crops.
- ◆ **Moon in Aquarius:** Cultivate, turn your soil, weed.
- ◆ **Moon in Pisces:** This is very fruitful. Plant anything that requires strong roots to grow abundantly.

Just for the fun of it, try one of these ideas out. Select a type of plant you want to cultivate during a specific moon phase and do just that. Hold the soil and seed in the moonlight so they absorb the energy. If you're going to use this plant for a particular magickal purpose, whisper that purpose to the seed so it knows your goal. Continue to do this each time you water and tend the plant. Make notes along the way in your magickal diary to see if you feel, as the ancients did, that the timing helped your plant's growth. If so, do it on a larger scale with any of the aforementioned gardens.

Crystal Gardening

Witches love crystals and stones. Each is like a little treasure with a pocket of energy housed inside. The ancient magickians certainly knew this when they used green agate to encourage crop growth, and there's no reason why the modern magick user can't follow that example.

There are several ways you can apply crystal gardening techniques. One is by simply placing a green agate, jade, moonstone, or magnet in the soil. Each of these stones is believed to promote plant growth. Or, you might choose a crystal that's more closely attuned to the plant's designated magickal purpose, such as planting a pink quartz beneath a rose bush to support loving energies.

A third alternative is that of keeping larger stones near your planters to surround the greenery with supportive energy. Finally, my personal favorite is that of stringing crystals and hanging them above the gardening area so the plants grow toward the light and the magickal energy you're hoping to create.

ACTIVITY: Banishing Bugs

For this activity you'll need to prepare a tea of catnip, coriander, nasturtium petals, tansy, marigold, rue, onion, garlic, tomato leaves, sage, and/or thyme. The basic proportion for this tea are 4 oz. of herb (any combination of herbs that totals 4 ounces) steeped in 8 oz. of warm water. The stronger the aroma, the better the results. Keep this stored in the refrigerator if you don't use it all right away. If it turns cloudy, however, discard it, as the mix has gone bad, and therefore, the magick won't work.

It's best to prepare this during a waning moon to inspire banishing. Stir the mixture counterclockwise as you work adding an incantation such as:

"BUGS BE GONE, ONLY HELPFUL ONES STAY,

BY MY WILL GO AWAY!"

Sprinkle this over your garden, again moving counterclockwise. Repeat this process if the garden gets wet (from rain) or when you notice the aroma diminishing.

ACTIVITY: Land Blessing

Consider timing this activity for April 13, when Romans blessed their fields. Go to your garden or window-sill planter and sprinkle a bit of wine and grain into the soil. (White or red wine is okay, but red wine accents life by its color.) Invoke your patron god or goddess if you wish, while moving (or dancing) clockwise around the area. Add an incantation such as this:

"IN THE EARTH I SOW, MY MAGIC TO GROW!

BRING ABUNDANCE TO THE LAND UPON WHICH I STAND."

You'll have to adjust this a bit for an indoor planting.

Repeat the incantation each time you tend your plants or the soil to further support the magick.

Urban Herbal Witchery

Green Witchery and herbalism often go hand in hand. The world is rapidly becoming aware of the positive effects that herbs can have on health and well-being. Green Witches have always known this, and often combined that knowledge with magickal methods to improve the effects.

If I told you that learning basic herbalism or magickal herbalism was a snap, I'd be misleading you. It takes time and research to become really good at it, because you have to become aware of holistic applications, metaphysical correspondences, and preparation techniques. Even more importantly, you need to attune yourself to each plant's spirit so you know how to use it most effectively in any setting.

The power, strength, and potential magickal applications for any plant can change dramatically depending on its growing conditions. The amount of water, sunlight, and minerals in the soil can all affect the energies any one plant bears, and only that plant can tell you its secrets!

Getting to Know Herb Spirits

How do you get to know a plant's secrets? The best way is through the spirit of that plant or through an Earth deva (an Elemental being) associated with that plant. Shamans have long used this method to learn which bits of greenery were best used to heal, bless, and energize their efforts.

To begin, take time getting to know the plant in question. Watch it grow. Watch the way its color and vitality change with water levels and sunlight. Keep it near you for several weeks. This will help you tune into the plant simply by osmosis.

Next, set up a sacred space and begin to meditate with the plant in front of you. Extend your hands gently toward the plant as if welcoming an old friend. Now comes the hard part: waiting. Wait to see if you get an empathic impression or physical sensation that symbolically or literally gives you clues as to this plant's best applications. For example, a plant that feels "hot" might be used to warm a cold heart, whereas a "cold" plant might be applied in magick for calming a heated temper. All these messages and more come from the plant's spirit when we slow down long enough to listen with all our natural and supernatural senses.

Harvesting and Preserving Magick

Once you've built a strong rapport with plant spirits, you'll want to honor them in the way you harvest anything for magickal purposes. Tradition tells us that we should always use noniron implements (because iron drains magic), and that anything harvested on Midsummer's Day will contain more natural power.

Besides a general lack of abundant growing space, many of today's Witches also face a lack of storage space. So, after you harvest your magickal herbs, the chore of drying and storing them properly might seem a little difficult. I'd like to provide you with some suggestions here, as well as magickal methods to try to accent the energies at hand.

First, the more mundane matters. Grow or buy only those things that you readily use. Gather bark in early Spring or late Fall, roots in late Fall, seeds when ripe and fragrant, herbs when mature, and flower petals first thing in the morning. This ensures that the oils and attributes of each will be at their peak.

Next, look around your living space with a creative eye. Use the ceiling in a dry, well-ventilated room for drying herbs (via a net or bundles strung from one wall to another). A small amount of wall space or the inside of a door could house shelves for well-labeled jars. The inside of a door is preferable, actually, because it protects the herbs from direct light that can damage the potency of the herbal oils, and, by extension, the magickal energy within.

Now for the witchy flair. Put creative labels on your jars (for example, Fellowship Flowers for a blend that accents kinship created predominantly from flowers). Color code them so each matches the magickal energy within. Put a sympathetic crystal—one whose color and magickal correspondences match that of the plant, such as lavender being peaceful and amethyst being tranquility—in the bottom of the jar (along with another label just in case the first one comes off). At this point whisper an incantation into the jar (or other storage container). In this particular illustration, it might be:

"UNITY AND TRUST WITHIN THESE HERBS BIND,
WE SHALL BE OF ONE HEART AND ONE MIND!"

Put the cap or cover on to keep the magick safe within.

Some Readily Available Herbs

Here is a very brief list of my favorite herbs that are readily available for use in and around the home along with their magickal and remedial applications. If you plan to do a lot of green Witchery, I strongly advocate getting several books that include information that you can consider, compare, and contrast. Two good choices are *Herbal Magick* by Paul Beyerl and my book *The Herbal Arts* (see the Appendix for more information).

Alfalfa: Magickally used for providence. Remedially used for joint problems and vitamin deficiency.

Aloe: Magickally used for protection, beauty, victory, and peace. Remedially, a popular aid for minor burns.

Anise: Magickally used for safety, purification, awareness, and happiness. Remedially good for coughs and indigestion.

Basil: Magickally used for love, prosperity, healing relationships, courage, and fertility. Remedially used to calm the nerves and ease stomach cramps.

Barley: Magickally used for fertility and money magick. Remedially used as a beverage for convalescents.

Catnip: Magickally used for cat magic, friendship, and joy. Remedially used for colds and sleeplessness.

Chamomile: Magickally used for meditation and focus. Remedially used for calming.

Cinnamon: Magickally used for power, love, victory, and psychic power. Remedially used for an astringent or digestion.

Clove: Magickally used to dispel negativity, increase money, and protect from gossip. Remedially used for colds.

Daisy: Magickally used for sun magic and attracting love. Remedially used as a burn/bruise salve.

Dandelion: Magickally used for divination, hospitality, and message spells. Remedially makes a good tonic.

Fennel: Magickally used for purification, health, and prosperity. Remedially used as an appetite suppressant.

Ginger: Magickally used for energy, success, and improved relationships. Remedially used for indigestion and colds.

Garlic: Magickally used for weather magick, courage, banishing, and protection. Remedially used as a purgative and circulatory aid.

Horseradish: Magickally used to protect from evil. Remedially used as a poultice for aches and pains.

Lavender: Magickally used for longevity, rest, wishcraft, and peace. Remedially used to heal wounds and ease headaches.

Lemon: Magickally used for blessing, devotion, and cleansing. Remedially good for colds and gentle cleansing.

Marigold: Magickally used for prophesy, legal aid, revealing fairies, and psychism. Remedially used for flu, fever, and burn compresses.

Mint: Magickally used for prosperity, strength, and healing. Remedially use for hiccups, colds, flu, and asthma.

Nutmeg: Magickally used for vision, psychic awareness, and passion. Remedially used to improve digestion and circulation.

Oak: Magickally used for luck, longevity, power, and health. Remedially used as a gargle or to ease symptoms of dysentery.

Olive: Magickally used for wisdom, luck, and peace. Remedially used for constipation, colic, and bug bites.

Parsley: Magickally used for fulfillment, protection, habit breaking, and success. Remedially used for cramps and to ease urinary infections.

Pine: Magickally used for centering, cleansing, healing, productivity, and purification. Remedially used for pain and swelling.

Rose: Magickally used for love, friendship, luck, joy, and many other things. Remedially used as an overall tonic to improve resistance to sickness.

Rosemary: Magickally used to improve memory retention, bring sleep, and encourage youthful outlooks. Remedially used for stress, flu, and headaches.

Saffron: Magickally used for wind magic, inspiring passion, and easing depression. Remedially used for colds and insomnia.

Sage: Magickally used for fertility, wishcraft, and wisdom. Remedially used for compresses and dandruff.

Thyme: Magickally used for rest, psychism, energy, and courage. Remedially used as an antiseptic.

Willow: Magickally used for making wands, calling spirits, divination, and love. Remedially used for headaches and fever.

Please note that Witches do not disdain medical science. Until someone is proficient (preferably licensed) in remedial herbalism, herbal remedies should only be used as an adjunct to commonsense medical care and magickal herbalism used as an astral support unit in the quest for wholeness.

Recipes

With all this information in hand often comes an amazing temptation to putter in your kitchen. If you like to make things at home that are both Earth-friendly and not overly time-consuming as far as preparation, this section is one you'll want to flag for quick reference. While the recipes have very mundane applications, there's nothing stopping you from spicing things up with a little magick.

The Preparation Process

To bring Witchery into your herbal arts, you need only consider many of the methods already presented in this book. Specifically:

♦ Consider timing your creation process to take place during a beneficial astrological sequence.

♦ Stir clockwise to draw positive energy, counterclockwise for banishing or binding.

♦ Visualize while you work.

♦ Chant or incant while you work.

♦ Light candles whose colors represent your goal.

♦ Burn supportive incense.

♦ Add one or two herbs specifically for their magickal energies as long as the effect won't hurt the recipe.

♦ Bless, charge, and dedicate your mixture for its intended purpose.

♦ Store the preparation in a symbolic container or label it creatively so that the whole package sings of your Witchery.

The Recipes

Air Freshener: Melt 1 cup of wax and add no more than 1/4 cup dried aromatic herbs and as much as 15 drops of essential oil to the base. Then mold this for burning or put it in a sunny place. For magickally clearing the air, I recommend lemon, orange, and pine.

Athlete's Foot: Soak the foot in a mixture of 1 cup warm cider vinegar, 1 gallon water, and 2 teaspoons thyme for 15 minutes. Rinse with the same mixture. (Rinsing feet regularly with this mixture is a good idea.)

Burns: Apply aloe vera gel or a blend of equal parts wheat flour, molasses, and baking soda.

Dandruff: Mix together 1 cup of peppermint, nettle, clover, and rosemary. Warm 1 cup herbs (any combination) to 2 cups water. Massage mixture into your hair using counterclockwise motions. Rinse.

Deodorant: Start with 1 cup corn starch and baking soda, to which 1 cup of orris root and 2 teaspoons of powdered orange peel, lemon peel, sage, and lavender have been added. These herbs have a cleansing and peaceful effect, too.

Facial: Simmer 2 cups of rose hips and 4 pieces of candied ginger in 1/4 cup of water until mushy. Strain and add 3/4 cup of sage honey to the liquid. Boil this slowly for 30 minutes, then cool and add 2 teaspoons aloe to the blend (to enhance mystical beauty). Dab this on in a thick layer then let it dry. Remove with warm water. Keep the remainder refrigerated as this makes about 8 masks. Note that this facial is edible and can be used as a jelly or sore throat treatment!

Flea Deterrent: Create this during the waning moon, about three weeks before the flea season begins in Spring, and continue treating the house during every waning moon until the season is well over. Make a tincture of penny-royal (4 oz. herb to 8 oz. alcohol). Dip your pet's collar in it and sprinkle the tincture liberally around its bed and any place it lays frequently.

Glue: Mix equal proportions of powdered rice and cold water. To this add another portion of boiling water until you get the right texture. Boil this for a minute on the stove. Add any herbs desired at this point to affix stones to wands, or whatever.

Itching: Make a poultice of 2 teaspoons each tansy, catnip, and vinegar.

Moths: During a waning moon mix up 1 teaspoon each pepper, tobacco, flour of hops, and salt with 4 ounces of cedar chips. Tie this into sachets and place them where the moths dwell.

Plant Fertilizer: Use this in your magickal garden, espe-cially if you make it during a full moon. To one gallon of warm water add one ounce nettle, two ounces comfrey root, and one ounce of kelp. Use regularly.

Rust Cleaner: Warm lemon juice, salt, and cream of tartar in equal proportions on the stove (low flame) until well mixed. Dab this on a cloth, then apply to the item in question. Try polishing in a counterclockwise pentagram to improve the banishing energy.

Skin Cream: Mix together 4 ounces of almond oil, a bit of may dew (if available, for magickal beauty), and 1/2 cup each of orange flowers, lemon grass, lavender, and a pinch of clove. Warm on the stove until the oil has the aroma, then strain. Add 1/2 cup wax and 2 teaspoons aloe gel. Remove from heat and beat it by hand, using a clock-wise motion, until creamy. Store in an airtight container. You can change the aromas in this to suit your magickal or emotional goals by simply changing the herbs you use.

Sleeplessness: Eat two raw onions before bed with a slice or two of bread and butter. If this isn't suited to your diet, try drinking a cup of valerian, catnip, peppermint, or chamomile tea instead.

Throat Infection: Gargle with a solution made from 1 cup of black tea in which 1/4 teaspoon each of lavender flower, salt, and vinegar have been added. Alternatively, try sage tea with honey and lemon.

Toothpaste: Mix one tablespoon baking soda with one teaspoon salt (protective), a cup of water, and a few drops of any personally preferred flavoring.

Vinegar: Open one batch of cider (vary the size of the batch according to your needs) and leave it in a sunny place with some garlic, dill, clove, allspice, mustard seeds, or other personally preferred spices therein. (Personal taste dictates how much you use of each herb; my personal preference is to add 1 garlic clove and 1/4 teaspoon of each dried herb per cup of vinegar.) Cover the top with a heavy cloth. In a month's time it will be spiced cider vinegar. You may wish to time this effort to begin on the waning moon so the cider "turns."

◆ ◆ ◆

It may take you awhile to get all the components necessary to make these kinds of recipes on a regular basis, and it doesn't need to be an ongoing hobby. Rather, practice green Witchery when your schedule permits as a celebration of creativity, your magickal skills, and the blessings of Earth. You'll find the end results are spiritually pleasing products that heal, bring joy to friends and family, and generate more magick in your life.

Chapter 5

Haggle and Hex

It is not so hard to earn money as to spend it well.
—Charles Spurgeon

Up to this point we've rebuilt ourselves and our environments, reconnected with the Earth, and poured healing energy into the web of life. What's still missing are the tools commonly employed by Witches in focusing, weaving, and releasing their magick in today's busy society.

Witchcraft is not unique among religions in that obtaining the right tools for the right job can quickly become expensive, especially in today's profit-driven world. Books, tapes, religious jewelry, and other paraphernalia fill gift shops, nature stores, and even the supermarket. This makes being an informed, aware, magickal consumer more difficult than one might initially expect. Which goods are really necessary and priced right? And which products are just scams to get a piece of the New Age pie?

I strongly feel that spirituality should not depend on the size of a Witch's pocketbook, nor should the quest for enlightenment be derailed by moneychangers. This chapter's purpose is to help all Witches discern which merchants have the best products and the best intentions, and to show how we can make or find our magickal tools at reasonable prices by using reason, haggle or barter, and old-fashioned spellcraft.

How to Sue Your Spirit Guide

I have often joked that I was somewhat uncomfortable in trusting channeled information in that you can't exactly go back to a Spirit and ask for accountability. New Age has become big business—but not all Witches have a big budget to match. Thankfully, in the Witch's market, a big price tag isn't always the key to a well-loved, powerful magickal implement.

Witchcraft is rarely listed in the phone book's yellow-page directory, so many Witches still find themselves having to depend on gatherings, mail order, the Internet, and other means of purchasing, not all of which ensure our satisfaction or protection from fraud. This has led me to developing a system that I've found quite helpful in weeding out some of the best choices for magickal goods and services.

I recommend asking yourself the following questions before making a purchase:

♦   Does the company make impossible claims, such as ensuring their spells work 100 percent of the time? Such a claim should send up a red flag in your mind. No responsible Witch would ever say that, knowing how personal magick can be.

♦   In catalogs or on Web sites, are pictures of the products unclear or distorted? If so, there may be a good reason in terms of quality, or the company may be attempting to misrepresent a product's size.

- How is the product priced compared to similar products? It is one thing to feed your family and pay bills, but it's another thing altogether to live the "high-life" by marking prices up and thus preying on people's desire for spiritual experiences.

- Does the merchant, serviceperson, or group offer sliding scale fees or barter for those with justifiable financial constraints? The Association for Research and Enlightenment offers reduced workshop rates when people prove their need. Similar practices speak volumes for the intentions of any business.

- What kind of philosophy does the company portray in advertising? Is it more hocus-pocus than real, modern magick? If so, you might want to look elsewhere. An excellent example of a company that operates with good advertising is Earth Care Paper Products. This company has a no-nonsense mailing that includes useful consumer information on Earth-friendly practices. This, to me, reflects the right focus for their business.

- What type of guarantee does the company/individual offer? Does it provide refunds or exchanges? If not, beware. Anyone who offers goods and services for a fee needs to be accountable for customer service too.

- Does the merchant answer your questions reasonably or do they shift into "salesperson" mode? You may quickly discover a treasure or a complete sham just by using your magickal skills.

- How knowledgeable do the company's representatives seem? If I called a purportedly magickal store in search of items for moon magick, for example, I'd get nervous if the reply was, "What's moon magick?"

- Has the company been recommended by anyone you know and trust? In the magickal community, word-of-mouth advertising is among the most reliable sources of information.

If, after reviewing these questions, you come up with two or more potential outlets for what you need, you can then return to your Witchery for aid:

♦ Put the names of the merchants/servicepeople in a pendulum circle drawn on paper and then divining for the best choice. For this, put your elbow down on the table's surface in such a way so the pendulum point sits directly in the middle of the circle. Close your eyes and focus on the item/price range you need. When you feel the pendulum moving, see which of the stores it points out.

Alternatively, if you have business cards for the stores in question you can simply shuffle them upside down while keeping your goal in mind. Then, pick out one card as you might a daily tarot card. Start at that store first.

♦ Create an amulet for guidance and discernment. For example, hold a piece of coral or jade (for wisdom) and empower it, saying:

"INSIDE THIS STONE, MY MAGICK BIND,

HELP ME IN ____ TO FIND." [fill in the blank with the name of the tool/item for which you're looking].

Then, tuck this in your pocket and visit the store(s) you've chosen. Touch the stone, extend your psychic skills to the tool(s) in question. Which ones appeal to both your higher senses and your budget?

♦ If you find something you really want and that draws your spiritual senses strongly but you cannot afford, try this spell. Get a bunch of candied almonds (for prosperity) and fill them with magick using an incantation such as this:

"GOD/DESS SEE MY WISH AND BLESS, BRING TO ME
    ABUNDANCE!

IF THIS _____ IS TO BE MINE, FIND A WAY FOR MY MAGICK
TO SHINE!"

Eat one or two of these candies regularly to internalize the energy necessary to generate either enough income to cover the object, have it go on sale, or come to you some other way (perhaps as a gift).

Because Wicca is becoming big business, remember that your merchants have a responsibility to you. They have to follow commonly accepted business practices just like any other business. Anyone you feel may be presenting fraudulent, misrepresented, or otherwise improper goods should be confronted with your concerns. If you find those concerns are justified, do something about it! Expose misdeeds through the Better Business Bureau or your local chamber of commerce, remembering that such individuals reflect badly on Witches as a whole and rob us of precious opportunities to re-educate the public about our faith.

The Budget Guru

Most Witches find that they slowly collect the tools and components with which they work. Over the years the exact composition of this magickal tool kit changes to match the individual's growth. But as we obtain or change our tools, the bottom line still comes into play, especially when our budgets don't always have a lot to spare. This leaves modern Witches with two choices: We can either learn to make what we need or find what we need at the right price.

ACTIVITY: The Goodwill Goddess

I have a friend who's taken this idea to a whole new level. She calls it supplicating the Goodwill Goddess. Her favorite places to shop for magickal implements are secondhand stores, flea markets, and junk shops. But since the Goodwill Goddess can be a "hit or miss" proposition, she uses the spell that follows here before going shopping.

For the spell you'll need four quarters. Hold these in your strong hand and say:

"MY PENNY'S SAVED, A _____ TO EARN,

WITHIN THESE COINS LET MAGIC BURN!"

Fill in the blank with the item you're seeking. Take these coins with you and use them in parking meters that are about to expire or for other similar acts of kindness. This will help manifest your wish and neatly bless others in the process.

ACTIVITY: Haggle and Barter

For those merchants with whom you know there's some pricing leeway, you can use this spell to try to improve your chances of getting a good deal. The components for this spell are a large feather and a bowl of 1 cup of mead to which a pinch of mint has been added. These ingredients inspire communication skills and congeniality. Hold the bowl in one hand and the feather in the other while standing outside. Turn to the East and say:

"MAGICKAL POWER OF MINTED MEAD,

BRING SUCCESS IN TODAY'S DEEDS!"

Dip the feather in the mead and sprinkle it out. Continue turning clockwise, adding other incantations that further indicate or support your goals, such as:

"I GIVE THIS LIQUID TO THE WINDS,

LET THE MAGICK NOW BEGIN!"

When you finish, facing North, pour the rest of the mead to the Earth by way of libation.

Make It Yourself

If you decide to create your own tools, I think you'll find the effort well worth the time. The final product will be filled with personal energy and you'll probably have more insights into that item's symbolic value by working so closely on it. In the following section are instructions for making several commonly desired items for the magickal household. When you're done, consider how the process of making the item affected both you and that object. Note the experience and insights gained in your magickal diary.

Finding and Making Magickal Tools

This section includes not only recipes and instructions, but also alternatives and ideas on where to shop for the time-challenged Witch. By employing a wise combination of these methods, you can make or find magickal regalia that fall well within your budget and still sing the song of your soul!

Aromatherapy and Anointing Oil

Because of the growing popularity of aromatherapy, I highly suggest finding a wholesale outlet for essential oils; the mark-up at bath and body stores is horrendous! In particular, I'd recommend getting a catalog from Frontier Herbs, whose prices are fantastic. You can reach Frontier Herbs at (800) 669-3275.

For those who wish to make oils, the process isn't too difficult, but it does require a little patience. Begin with a good base oil, such as virgin olive, almond, or saffron. (These cost a little more, but they also have a longer shelf life.)

I recommend making one-cup quantities of oil at a time. This way you'll have enough for several months, but not so much that it costs a fortune to make. Warm the oil and add one teaspoon of each herb desired. If you're using flowers, be very careful about the temperature of the oil. Too much heat will result in a very unpleasant smell.

Steep your herbs until you're pleased with the aroma. If necessary, strain and add fresh herbs to achieve the desired potency. Some herbs take longer to integrate into the oil, particularly rosins and woods. Cooking spices, on the other hand, are great choices for people with a hectic schedule, because they produce nearly immediate results. Do be careful, however, with cinnamon, cloves, and other strong aromatics, as these can irritate your skin if using them for massage or anointing. Use them judiciously, considering other possible alternatives that aren't as volatile, such as orange.

Hint: When you're first starting to make your own oils, use simple recipes with no more than three additives. It becomes very difficult to balance and blend the energies and aromas from many base components successfully. You can always mix and match these with other oils you've prepared to achieve different magickal results. Also, don't forget to time this process for propitious moon phases or other astrological factors, adding old-fashioned kitchen Witchery to your work, such as stirring clockwise to attract "good vibes."

Belts

For those of us who enjoy wearing ritual robes, belts are indispensable. Not only do they provide a spot to which to tie tools, but they are a perfect place to secure one's skirts for enthusiastic ritual dancing!

Finding a variety of belts is certainly easy enough at clothing stores and secondhand shops. If you prefer to make your own, however, you have many options. You could buy a leather working kit, you could sew a belt out of a personally pleasing length of fabric, or you could braid one out of colored cords (similar to those used to hold back curtains).

This last option presents a perfect opportunity for you to weave in some magick while you create. As you get to the area where all three strands cross, incant a spell and/or tie in a symbolic object (such as a seashell, feather, bell, or beads). This way the belt becomes a representation of the Sacred Circle and the Elements!

Candles

Hobby shops often carry beeswax in large amounts for candle-making, as well as molds. Otherwise, you might want to save the drippings from candles used for specific spells and rituals separated out by that function (for example, love, health, or money). When you have enough to remelt, you can then add herbs, tiny shells and stones, or essential oils before pouring into a mold (provided by an old quart-size milk container or an ice cube tray). What's nice here is that your Witchery has already saturated the wax with power. The herbs and other ingredients simply augment that power, which is then released when you light your candle!

Cauldrons

Old farm and country shops still carry such items. Or, if you don't mind a substitute without the feet attached, just get yourself a good iron pot and season it properly. When you're camping out at Wiccan events, these pots can be safely placed on tripods over the ritual fire (making the traditional cauldron appearance).

Crystals

The best sources for crystals are, by far, college geology departments and rock and mineral shows. While museum and gift shops carry them, the prices are usually much higher than necessary. One particular outlet that I recommend for good prices is Lotus Light/Blue Pearl. You can reach them at (800) 822-4810. They have a large variety of tumbled stones, points, and so on in varying sizes that can be purchased by the pound.

Cups

If you're in need of a homemade ritual cup, how about a large seashell that's been boiled clean, a stoneware coffee mug, a drinking horn, or a wooden goblet? You might also try drying a gourd and treating it with a safe, waterproof coating. To buy one, try secondhand shops or gift shops.

God and Goddess Images

Your first stop for one of these images should be a lawn and garden shop. Lately I've noticed several pieces of statuary used for landscaping suited to the world's pantheons in these places. For a smaller image, try Eastern import shops and historically centered catalogs.

For those wishing to make an image yourself, you can sew poppets filled with herbs or flowers sacred to your patron/ness. Or, perhaps you could make salt dough images. The recipe for salt dough is one cup each salt, flour, and water. Knead the ingredients together for 10 minutes. Shape and bake at 325 degrees for one to two hours. (Cooking time varies based on the size of your image.) Glaze, paint, or adorn the image in a suitable way after it's cool. This is a fun project for children.

Herb Pillows and Sachets

Some of the easiest bundles you can create are those made from drawstring bags or heat-sealing tea bags. Choose your components, and then tie or seal the magick within. If you're using bags, pick out a color that augments your goal and draw a magickal symbol on the outside that also represents the sachet's purpose. These little bundles can go just about anywhere from clothing drawers (to charge your wardrobe with positive energy) to areas where nasty odors reside.

Herb pillows require a little more effort. Begin with a piece of fabric twice the size you want the finished pillow to be. Fold it in half. Stitch along two sides, leaving the last side open. Next, take some formed cotton batting the same size as the pillow. Wrap the batting around the herbs. A pillow for well-being might be filled with pine, mint, lemon rind, chamomile, and fennel. Spread this mixture out evenly so it's not bumpy, and sew the edge of the padding so it doesn't fall out. Slide this into the opening of the fabric.

Finally, iron under both unfinished sides of the pillow, about 1/4 inch. Stitch it shut, and you can add lace or other symbolic decorations to make the pillow visually pleasing and magickally meaningful.

Incense and Burners

You can find ready-made incense burners almost everywhere these days, including the supermarket. For those of you who may need a handy substitute in a pinch, I'd suggest a stoneware dish filled with dirt or sand. This allows you to safely put self-lighting charcoal and powdered incense within to burn, because the sand or soil absorbs the heat and holds the charcoal securely.

Homemade incense can be devised from any number of base materials. I suggest gathering wood shavings (perhaps from a friend's fireplace if you don't have one) as your base because these burn well and evenly. To these you can add dried flower petals, kitchen spices, rosins, and/or dried fruit rind. Use whatever quantities you prefer to create the desired magickal effect and aroma.

As with aromatic oils, don't try to mix too many things into your base at first. You can always adjust later. If you find that you can't get a strong enough aroma from using plant matter, add a few drops of essential oil to your blends. Shake thoroughly and make sure the blend dries so that no mold results.

Two combinations that I personally enjoy are rose, cinnamon, and myrrh for harmony and love; and lavender flowers, myrrh, mint, and just a bit of cinnamon for peace and relaxation.

Meditation Aids

Gongs, prayer bowls, and bells are all known to help center our spirits and improve focus for meditative work. For inexpensive bells in particular I recommend fabric and craft stores.

Another neat meditation aid is a miniature zen garden. Assemble it by finding any small wooden box (such as those that hold wine). Get some play sand at a toy store, or gather it at a beach. Fill the box 3/4 full. Add a few plain rocks or crystals.

When you want to meditate, start tracing symbols in the sand, or making patterns out of the crystals. Move slowly and purposefully, allowing the activity to draw you in deeper. When you feel relaxed and centered stop, close your eyes, and then continue on from there!

Pentagrams

You can buy pentagrams in many places today, ranging from jewelry stores to stained glass outlets. One online source with amazing prices is Whispered Prayers. These folks run a great shop with far more than just pentagrams! The Web site address is *www.whisperedprayers.com*.

For a more natural appeal, I suggest tying together fallen branches using colored ribbons to represent the Elements. Once assembled, you can then decorate this gift of nature with tiny items suited to the season or celebration at hand. Some suggestions are to put a colored candle in the middle and set it on your altar, to hang tinsel off it for Winter rituals, or to add fresh flowers for Beltane.

Robes

Look for old choir robes and caftans at secondhand shops. Many of these can be converted into really comfortable and visually pleasing ritual robes with little, if any, effort. Individuals who sew can make an oversized T-tunic that gets belted. (These are nice because they go together quickly, needing only a few seams.) Or, more simply still, pick out some special clothing that you'll keep aside only for ritual. No one ever said you *have* to wear robes. Wear whatever makes you feel witchy and what puts you in the right mental space for working magick.

Runes

If you're looking for a highly portable divination system with roots in antiquity, runes are a good choice because many people can use them effectively. You can make your own set using beach stones, shells, a blank set of cards, wood slices, or clay as a base. Treat your surfaces by cleaning (or sanding) them, if necessary, and then paint on or carve out the rune symbols. Use some kind of art spray or other finish to protect the tool from wear and tear. For example, you might treat wood slices regularly with lemon oil to avoid cracking and wear.

If you want to buy runes instead of making them, try a bookstore or a New Age store.

Smudge Sticks

If you can get long cuttings of sage, lavender, cedar, pine, or sweetgrass, you can make your own bundles at home. Gather your herbs so that your pointer finger and thumb just reach around the grouping. At the top, take several pieces of sympathetically colored threads and begin wrapping tightly. Each color has a magickal value. Red represents life, energy, love, and safety. Yellow is for communication, creativity, and fertility. Green inspires growth, gradual maturity, and healing. Blue is peaceful, gentle, and happy. Purple has strong spiritual overtones and connects with leadership abilities. White is the color of Spirit and protection.

Once the top is secured, you can criss cross the thread down the length of the smudge stick, knotting at each cross mark. Don't forget to bind a spell there, such as:

"IN THIS BUNDLE OF SAGE AND PINE,
PURITY AND CLEANSING BIND."

Let this dry thoroughly before burning for purification and cleansing. Burn only what you need, then douse the end in water to make sure the bundle is safely put out.

You can find smudge sticks in New Age shops, herb shops, and Native American stores.

Tarot Cards

I've come up with some really fun ideas for making my own tarot decks in recent years out of mediums that can be found around the house. The first is making a deck out of greeting cards whose covers (back images) are the same size. All you need to do is collect enough cards that equate to the tarot's symbolism (72) and treat the paper with an art spray for longevity. Second, how about using equally sized grocery coupons? Back these on poster board for a sturdier medium.

If you're handy at drawing or painting, get a blank deck of cards (or blank 3 x 5 cards) and begin designing your own deck that way. This approach can also work for decoupage decks where you cut out the images you want from magazines and apply them to the surface of the card. Nature lovers might secure pressed flowers, seeds, and leaves similarly.

If you want to buy a deck of tarot cards, your first stop should be a bookstore.

Wands

Wands can be purchased at a New Age shop or a magick store. Often, though, it's more fun to make your own.

Clay, wood, and metal all make good bases for magickal wands. For example, you can get a length of copper tubing at a hardware store, adhere a crystal to one end, and have a very serviceable wand for guiding energy where you want it to go!

You could also get self-hardening clay and rub, twist, and turn it in any way you choose. Set crystals in the clay while it dries, or paint it after it's dry, to create symbolic decorating motifs.

My favorite type of wand, by far, is wooden. To make one yourself, take a walk in a nearby park watching for a gift from one of the trees lying on the ground. Trust me when I say you'll know which one is best for your Witchery. After you find it, soak the entire branch in water for several weeks to loosen the bark and make it easier to remove.

Once you remove the bark, either by sanding or peeling it, sand any rough edges so you won't get splinters later. Look for any good nooks and crannies into which you can set crystals. Carve these out a little bit using a sharp knife. Mix just a pinch of powdered myrrh into your glue to secure the chosen crystal in place. Finally, consider adding a hand-hold made from fabric that's held in place with ribbons. (This will make the wand more comfortable to hold.) Put a few beads at the end of the ribbon, or feathers to honor the Air element, and you're ready to go!

Temperate Technomagick

Today's Witches don't see technology as magick's adversary, but rather as a potential helpmate. And because we have tons of gadgets around us all the time, we might as well put them to good use as part of our savings sorcery! How? Simply start considering them as potential spell and ritual components, visualization symbols, and/or tools in a manner that's meaningful considering the way they're applied in everyday life. Here are some examples that will save you both time and money in your Witchery:

Blender

Use it to bring harmony, consistency, or coherence to beverages, incense, or other spell components. For example, to improve accord in your marriage, make a potion consisting of two cups of milk, a banana, a touch of anise, and a hint of cinnamon. Blend to "whip up" the magick!

Coffee Pot

Perk up stamina, potency, and energy in every pot of coffee you brew. Add 1/2 tsp. culinary spices for more specific magick, such as a hint of ginger and cinnamon to enhance the coffee's energetic effect.

Computer

I keep my Book of Shadows on computer. Each file is saved under a symbolic name so each time I open the file I can symbolically retrieve that energy into my life. Beyond that, you can use a blank computer screen for scrying, old memory chips in remembrance spells, a piece of the central processing unit as a component for reasoning spells, keyboards for communication, and the like.

Fax Machine

When you want to transmit your magick over long distances, why not use a fax? Draw a symbolic image of the energies you've created through ritual or spell work, then send it out to a friend in need! When the fax arrives, the printing process releases your magick directly into the recipient's hands!

Internet

There is no greater way to network and gather information than the Internet. There are countless Web sites, chat rooms, and groups for Witches.

Light Bulbs

Light bulbs are the modern equivalent of candles. You can buy them in a variety of colors to bring various vibrations into the sacred space of home, or dab them with aromatherapy oils to release those energies into the air. Keep a firm image of your goal in your mind as you approach the lamp, then turn it on to literally "light up" the magick! If you want to add an incantation to the process, do so just before turning the knob.

Microwave

When you need your magick to manifest more quickly, this is an excellent tool to use, provided that your components are microwave-safe. You do not have to warm the ingredients very long, because the microwave excites the individual molecules in them, which also ignites the magick and gets it moving toward your goal speedily.

Music

Music has been around for thousands of years, but modern technology has made it more accessible and given us wider varieties from which to choose. When you want to set just the right mood for magick, play a CD created by your favorite New Age artist. Or, if you feel creative, pick out a song whose tune you like and substitute new words to it that fit its beat. This is called "filking" and it can be really fun to try.

Some of the longest-standing examples of filking are the many witchy verses that have been added to the gospel song "Old Time Religion." These two, which I cannot attribute to an author, will nonetheless give you the gist of the idea:

Variety's life's spices
When gods of old entice us
Just Ankh if you love Isis
She's good enough for me!

or

With your trusty old athame
You can cast a double whammy
Or slice and dice salami.
That's good enough for me!

A more serious and lovely illustration was given me by a pen pal, Janella. It goes to the tune "'Tis a Gift to be Simple." This is a lovely example of how to adapt any piece of music you know to suit your vision or a magickal goal, and all you need is your voice to do it!

I will go into the Circle in the Spring of the year,
with my arms full of flowers and my heart full of cheer.
I will go into the Circle in the Spring of the year
and sing our Lady's praises.
I will go into the Circle when the Summer is nigh.
I will dance in the grove while the full moon's in the sky.
I will go to the Circle when the Summer is nigh
and sing our Lady's praises.

I will go into the Circle when Autumn leaves are brown,
joyful in the blessings of the harvest which abounds.
I will go to the Circle when the Autumn leaves are brown
    and sing our Lady's praises.
I will go into the Circle when the Winter snow is deep,
across the frozen mountains, dreaming in their sleep
I will go to the Circle when the Winter snow is deep
    and sing our Lady's praises.

Paint Roller/Sprayer

Any time you need to apply a fresh layer of paint to a wall, why not roll on some magick with it? The roller smoothes and evens the paint, making it a marvelous symbol of harmony. Your focus alone can make all the difference, but if you want to add more sensual support, put a few drops of aromatic oil in the paint. It won't harm the consistency, but it will leave a pleasing aroma in the room and express your magickal intentions without words until you paint again.

Refrigerator/Freezer

Want to slow down a relationship, or freeze some negativity that's aimed in your direction? Put an emblem of the relationship inside the refrigerator or freezer. Additionally, you might put consumable components in here before eating or drinking them for keeping a cool head, tempering heated arguments, or calming down a relationship that's gotten too hot, too quickly.

Stove

The modern version of the hearth, the stove is the heart of your home. Somewhere nearby keep an image of your house god/dess and provide bits of your food to the image to promote ongoing blessings. The pilot light in a gas stove additionally represents the never-ending love in the home. Whatever you make here (or in the oven) is filled with warmth and other good feelings. I strongly suggest you never cook when you're angry or out of sorts, because that negativity can transfer into the food and ruin the wonderful magick that abides there.

◆ ◆ ◆

I'm sure if you look around your home you can find many other bits of technomagick just waiting for your inventive touch. Staplers might be used for bonding and security spells. The kitchen sink can become the Water element in a ritual. A washing machine represents purification and cleansing (and you can add some herbal teas to improve the effect). Really, the options are nearly endless. And with technology continuing to grow, I believe it will continue to be a cost-effective, powerfully symbolic option as we practice our magick in the modern world.

Chapter 6

Do-It-Yourself Psychic

Let it be discovered by divination, or let a divinely inspired man declare it.

—Hittite prayer of Mursil II

L iving successfully and spiritually in this world requires a lot of witchy ingenuity. Our senses are barraged every moment of every day with noise, ideas, conversations, commercials, and other types of input. This leaves less and less space and time for us to key into our psychic, magickal selves for guidance and insights. This is a condition that I feel needs to change so we can really begin blending magick into daily reality in transformational ways.

Wake up That Psychic!

Having a solid spiritual foundation combined with heightened psychic awareness creates a powerful partnership for magickal and personal fulfillment. But many of us have found that just because one is a Witch, that doesn't always mean one is psychically aware. Practicing magick *helps*, but psychic attunement is a discipline all its own. These abilities require some work on our part to wake them up and keep them activated in spite of distractions.

Many of the activities provided in Chapters 1 and 2 will help you begin the process of awakening your inner psychic, or giving it a much-needed tune-up. Those offered here then become maintenance kits—little helpmates when you notice your senses aren't as keen as you might wish.

ACTIVITY: Reach Out and Touch Something

With time and practice this activity will allow you to develop the skill of psychometry (object reading) with just about anything in which you come in contact. When you're looking for magickal tools, this ability helps you find exactly the right ones that mingle with your personal energies in a beneficial way. (Most people find being in close proximity to an item or person improves their spiritual awareness of that item or person.) As a result, you're bound to be more prepared for what's about to happen, thanks to the information/insights you gain.

For this activity you'll need to assemble a grouping of small objects, both natural (such as a leaf or flower) and man-made (such as a pen or a coin). Put these on an empty surface in front of you. Now, close your eyes for a minute, center yourself, and relax. Drift into a gentle meditative mindset.

Next, reach out with your strong hand, palm down, over any one of the items. Do you feel anything? Do you receive any mental images or hear anything? Wait a few minutes and see. Remember, even if an object is man-made, it has an astral presence that we can interpret with our higher senses.

Now, switch hands. Do you find you feel or sense anything differently now? What about with both hands at once? Purpose-fully extend your aura so that it embraces the object. How has your understanding of it changed? Continue this way with a couple more items, mixing natural with man-made.

Cue the Psychic

In my years of working on psychic development I've often found that having some sensual cues, or portable tokens, helps the process along. Basically, you make a power pouch, talisman, or charm that represents your psychic self in fully activated form and keep it with you as a touchstone. When you need that aspect of self, you rub that touchstone to stir up the right magick in your aura for unlocking your inner psychic.

To give you a personal example, I use a small herbal oil container as my touchstone. It contains a homemade blend of frankincense and myrrh that was prepared during the full moon (representing a similar fullness in intuitive senses). Each time I'm going to do a reading, or use my psychic senses for something, I dab a bit of this on my third eye, the seat of psychic activity. Over time this mini-ritual has become a cue to my higher senses that says, "Hey, wake up. You're needed now!"

Try making something similar for yourself. It could be a bundle of herbs, a crystal or two, a piece of jewelry you wear only during readings, a special cloth upon which you put your tarot cards, or whatever. Whatever you choose, make sure it's something you can have handy as needed, and that immediately reminds you of the spiritual task you're about to undertake. Work with this cue for six months, noting your progress in your magickal diary. I think you'll find it becomes an excellent tool and partner for your psychic development and improved insights.

Choosing the Right Tool for You

The New Age market has been very kind to Witches in providing hundreds of psychic tools from which to choose. And while you don't need a tarot deck or pendulum kit to activate your psychic self, tools often make it easier. Basically a tool gives you a medium upon which to focus your attention, decreasing the sense of self-doubt that might come with simply declaring a prediction without any such medium. Effectively, when we stop feeling self-conscious about our skills, it helps release the inner psychic, with a resounding "Aha!"

The question then becomes: Which tool should you choose? Visual people will probably want something like the tarot, while tactile people seem to like runes or crystal castings. Consider which of those two senses you respond most strongly to so you can gear your search accordingly.

The next step is to explore what's available at stores, magickal friends' homes, and gatherings. Don't make a quick decision. Wait until the psychometric skill or other intuitive sense you've developed indicates a good choice.

Once you choose a tool, practice using it for several months. See how successful your readings are, and how personally mean-ingful the symbols become. Remember to use the cue you've made, and prepare yourself through meditation or other little rituals for the task at hand (whether it be lighting candles/ incense, prayer, fasting, or something else). Most people find this trial period dramatically confirms or denies the choice of psy-chic helpmate.

Portable Prophets

Witches are a tool unto themselves when it comes to psychism, but having external mediums puts less strain on the reader, and makes the whole process more user-friendly. So, as time goes on and your intuitive senses continue to grow, you're going to want to have some divination tools that are readily por-table. After all, our society is tremendously mobile, and nearly everyone I know insists on taking at least one tool with him or her on the road!

In that spirit, I'd like to provide you with some instructions here on using everyday items for fortune telling. Even if you haven't remembered to bring a preferred system with you to augment psychic abilities, you can try adapting something on hand!

Beans

Buy a bag of mixed dry beans at the supermarket. Take a handful and hold them while thinking about your question. When you have a firm image of the question in mind, release the beans to a plain-colored surface (white is best, because it's easy to see things against it). Now, look at the patterns made by the beans. Pretend you're trying to find a shape in an ink blot. If you were asking about a relationship and the resulting pattern was a heart, for example, this would be regarded as a positive sign.

An alternative way to use beans is to get similarly sized ones in a variety of colors and assign a meaning to each one. For example, a red bean could mean stop, a black bean could be a negative response, a white bean is traditionally positive, yellow beans might reveal a need for creativity or communication, and a green bean can symbolize a favorable omen for new projects. Put all the beans in a bag so you can focus on your question, then draw out one in answer to that question. Again, the beans must be of nearly equal sizes so as to ensure the randomness of your choice or the results will be tainted.

If you can't find beans, a good substitute is colored hard candies, which are often available at hotel gift shops, gas stations, supermarkets, and many other places.

Buttons

You can often find a variety of buttons at supermarkets, craft stores, fabric shops, and the like. As with the beans, you'll need to make sure the buttons you select are of similar sizes and assign a meaning to each one. You can use color symbolisms as those given for beans, or possibly assign values according to the visual pattern on the button.

If you decide to cast the buttons onto a surface rather than picking one or two from a bag for interpretive values, you'll need to consider both their color/patterns and where they land. The closer the button lands to you, the more personal the information and the sooner that situation will come to pass. Things landing to the left usually indicate a negative, while those on the right are a positive. So, if you decided a blue button meant happiness but it landed close to you on the left, the portent is one of some glitch in the not-too-distant future that may cause you some sadness.

When all else fails, if you have a button-down shirt and your question can be answered with a yes or no, old lore says you can use your shirt for an answer. Count the number of buttons holes. An odd number is a negative response; an even number is positive.

Charm Tokens

For this system you'll need to collect several small tokens (such as those from a board game or those found on charm bracelets). I suggest 13 in all so you have a reasonable diversity of interpretive values. Once you gather the tokens, determine in advance each one's meaning. For example, a tiny silver shoe might represent travel or walking a specific path, while an anchor could represent either security or things that hold you back.

Put the tokens in a pouch, think of a question, and gently shake the bag lightly with the top open. Whichever token falls out first represents your answer. If you need more clarification, keep shaking for a second or third token.

If you want to assemble this quickly, consider using household items, such as an eraser, a pack of matches, a key, or a battery, instead of charms. As before, give each a meaning. The eraser might represent mistakes that you still have a chance to fix, the matches a potentially hot situation, the key could symbolize opportunity, and the battery, personal energy. If you don't have a bag within which to shake the tokens, try scattering them on a square surface. Interpret the results this way:

- ◆ **Top center:** something halted or waiting.

- ◆ **Top right:** in the future, something that's beginning.

- ◆ **Middle right:** coming soon; something that offers hope or a new idea.

- ◆ **Lower right:** present; something in the works or full of energy.

- ◆ **Bottom center:** a very intimate matter that may be heated.

- ◆ **Lower left:** present; a problem to overcome.

- ◆ **Middle left:** soon; dwindling resources or energy for a project.

- ◆ **Upper left:** future; something that wanes, decreases, or shows signs of stagnation.

- ◆ **Center:** a central issue around which the entire question resolves, so look closely. Alternatively, something that has no real resolution right now.

Dice

Dice are marvelously portable, and nearly everyone has one or two extra lying around from board games. If you feel really flush, go to a gaming supply shop and get a special one just for fortune-telling efforts. You can get more detailed with these, because there are dice with up to 20 sides!

When a situation arises that needs some clarification or you need affirmation of a feeling, hold the die and concentrate. Visualize the matter at hand, specifically where you're uncertain about your instincts. When the die feels warm, roll it. Here's a sample of interpretive values for this system that you can certainly adapt to personal vision:

1: Singularity is needed. Don't scatter yourself, and trust your instincts.

2: Work in tandem with another. A friend or companion's insight proves valuable. Choices.

3: Creativity or diversification is the key to success.

4: Use logic and reason to work through the situation. Stay organized and mentally uncluttered.

5: Don't act on impulse. The desired changes are just around the corner so hold steady.

6: Love is important here, as is staying true to your ideals. Focus more on home.

Obviously if you have a die with more facets than six, or choose to use several six-sided dice, you'll need to expand this correspondence list. Consult any book on numerology for ideas.

Junk Drawer Divination

Almost everyone I know has a spot where miscellaneous junk gets put, whether it be a drawer, a glove compartment, a box, or some other place. This odds-and-ends collection makes a great medium for gaining insights into current or future matters. Why? Because they're already filled with personal energy, and there's a great variety of tokens to which to ascribe interpretive value.

To use the junk drawer system, you need only think of your question with your eyes closed. Reach into the drawer, keeping your question in mind. (No peeking!) Put your palm down over the top of the collection and scan the energy without physically touching anything. Wait until your palm feels itchy or warm, then grab what's underneath. Here are some potential interpretive values that I took from my own drawer:

Battery: The need to put energy into something or be careful about the way you're applying energy to a particular situation.

Die: Relying on chance or luck (for boon or bane). The number facing upward on the die might reveal more insights.

Hook: Catching something or putting your "hooks in."

Lighter: The spark of creativity; bringing renewed fire to a project that's gone cold.

Nail: Securing something, or "hammering home" an idea to yourself or someone else.

Pencil: Communication matters, possibly those that need correction.

Plug (three-way): Adaptability; being able to switch your focus and energy to something new as necessary.

Ribbon: Celebrations and fun surprises. Alternatively, the need to bind or release something/someone.

Tape: The need to clean up loose ends or figuratively pack up things you no longer need. Alternatively, a gentle form of constraint.

Tweezers: Stop picking everything apart! Get rid of the thorn, and move on.

Wire: Conducting yourself in a suitable manner, especially in the way you use energy. Alternatively, a stronger form of constraint.

Key Pendulum

I can never think of a time when I'm without a set of keys, so for me keeping an extra key just for fortune telling on my key chain is no great task. I get my pendulum keys at yard sales and flea markets because I like the antique-looking types with decorative tops—but really any key that's made with pre-drilled holes will work.

To use your key as a pendulum, I suggest cleaning it in a solution of 1 teaspoon salt (or lemon juice) to 2 cups water, so that it's free of random energy (old-fashioned soap and water is also fine). Next, take a piece of thread twice the length of the distance between your elbow and your wrist and put it through the key's hole. Knot the thread firmly.

Placing your elbow on a table, hold the topknot between your thumb and forefinger. Steady the key with your other hand so it's fairly still. Now close your eyes and think of a question. When you feel the key begin to move see what direction it's going, and use these interpretive values as starting points:

- **Up and down:** Yes.
- **Left to right:** No.
- **Hesitation or bobbing:** No answer is available/ uncertainty.
- **Circle:** The answer involves a man.
- **Oval:** The answer involves a woman.
- **Diagonals:** Conflicts or barriers.
- **Ellipse North/South:** Use your instincts.
- **Ellipse East/West:** Use logic and reason.

To give your pendulum work more interpretive values, place some of the charms you've gathered around the key in the shape of a circle. Watch to see if the key swings toward one of those symbolic tokens or between two of them to expand the meaningfulness. For example, if you've asked about a job decision and you observe an East/West ellipse that constantly touches on a silver boat, the meaning might be that you need to reason out your decision and that travel abroad or a move might be involved.

Omen reading

Omens and signs are mediums through which the Sacred Parent, Universal Powers, or our own Superconscious reaches out to give us a much-needed hint. The hint can come through any number of sources: an overheard phrase, a found object, a chance meeting, and the like.

The ancient omen observers, more often than not, turned to Nature and her citizens for most of omen observation. Today's Witch isn't always fortunate enough to have this realm readily available as a teacher and messenger, so we have to get a little creative in our techniques and begin paying attention to odd happenstance occurrences that may not be coincidental at all.

For example, say for an entire week you see elephants everywhere—in commercials, on business cards, on bulletin boards, at toy stores, even in your dreams! This might be an omen that you've forgotten something (elephants never forget) or that you're carrying around useless baggage (the proverbial white elephant).

You'll really have to trust your higher senses to discern the difference between flukes and true omens. I'm not one who believes that every moment in our lives has deep, spiritual significance. But, the more open you become to things like these, the more often you will receive messages this way simply by virtue of preparedness. Better still, omen reading requires no tools other than what your own senses provide!

Pen/Pencil

A pen or pencil represents another good option for today's Witch's divinatory tool kit—and something most people have with them all the time. You're going to do a little meditative doodling or writing. This doesn't require mediumistic skills as in traditional automatic writing. All you're going to do here is tap into your creative, insightful self and let it out through the pen or pencil.

Sit down where you can write comfortably and with as few interruptions as possible. Relax, take three deep breaths, and let all the tension drain out of your shoulders. When you feel comfortable, pick up the pen or pencil and put it on a piece of paper in front of you. Don't try to write or draw anything specific. If it helps, just make circles and dots for a while until you feel yourself being lead to write or draw more specifically. Your hand will seem to move of its own accord.

Continue this process until you naturally stop. Look to see what's in front of you. If it's an image, interpret it according to what you see in the imagery. If it's words, see what they have in common with your question, and what perspective they may offer that you haven't had before. We all really do know what's best for us deep down, but sometimes we need a way to tap into that knowledge. This particular divination system gives you just that, all in a common implement to any office, hotel, or home.

Tea and Coffee

This is far less messy than traditional tea-leaf reading. All you need is a cup of black coffee or tea and some cream. Drink 2/3 of your beverage while keeping your question strongly in your mind. Now pour in a dollop of cream and stir it once (only once) gently clockwise and see what images develop. Here's a sample list of interpretive values to try or adapt:

Circle: Cycles, or a connection that you've missed.

Cream rises toward the right of the cup: A good sign.

Cream sinks toward the left of the cup: A negative sign.

Cross: An important and difficult decision.

Diamond: A truly valuable thing that you may not wholly appreciate.

Dog: Remain devoted.

Eye: Use your insight; you already know the answer!

Flower: Something coming to fruition.

Hand: Accepting/giving assistance, friendship, or a promise.

Heart: Love or other matters of the heart.

Key: An opening or closing.

Letters: Initials of people involved in the question (also sometimes of places).

Line: A path to follow or something over which you should not cross.

Mask: Putting something on for the sake of appearances or hiding behind facades.

Numbers: Interpret according to numerological values.

Square: Foundations; getting closer to Earth.

Star: Hopes and wishes being fulfilled.

Tree: Reaching for a goal with good foundations in place.

X: Partnership or mutuality.

♦ ♦ ♦

If you'd like more information about divination and potential systems for your use and/or adaptation, I suggest reading *Futuretelling,* one of my books. In it you'll find more than 250 different fortune-telling systems, at least one of which will please your vision and help keep your psychic skills well-honed. (See the Appendix for more information.)

Symbols for the New Millennium

As discussed earlier in this chapter, if you're making a divination system of your own you may want to integrate more modern symbols such as the ones listed in this section. Why? Because as magick grows and changes alongside our world, our hallmarks also often transform. True, some archetypes in human awareness seem timeless, or minimally more adaptable to our times, but many other traditional symbols just don't function well because of societal/world changes. And, thanks to our being a global culture filled with technology, many potential symbols have no listed meanings in reference books because they didn't exist until very recently!

Timeless symbols such as the grail or sacred cup can certainly be left alone. No need to change what works! But you might want to find a more contemporary version of such an emblem. In this case a suitable symbol might be a picture of your favorite coffee mug!

Updating existing symbols is easier than defining wholly new emblems. For example, if you decided to make a Victorian-styled charm kit, it might include a glove. To the Victorians this represented propriety, but to us it's more strongly related with being very picky or detail-oriented (think of the "white glove" test to check for dust).

Then we come to creating a list of potential interpretations for the new things that have come into our lives, such as computers and spaceships. The spaceship might equate in earlier times to the horse—a means of movement, travel, of passing along messages—except on a much larger scale. The computer, however, is kind of unique. Creating our interpretive value for a tarot card whose illustration is a computer will depend heavily on what role that implement plays in our daily lives. For me, for example, it might represent creativity, organization, and networking. Making such highly personalized, meaningful choices in our symbols increases the magickal power they can provide.

Symbolic Interpretations of Modern Items

As you read this list, please bear in mind that there are many other symbols (animals, plants, crystals, colors, and so on) that you can consider for your magickal methods if they speak to your heart. But for today's world I felt it was important to focus this space on newer items that haven't really been considered much for their inherent symbolic value. Even at that, this list is very limited. It provides you with ideas that should fuel your own spiritual creativity in looking at the entire everyday working world as housing potential for magickal expression.

Also realize that in assembling this, I'm using gut instinct. As always, if the object/item means something different to you, that is the interpretation you should use and trust.

Air conditioner: Air Element; cooling; refreshment.

Airplane: Air Element; movement; bearing news or a specific type of energy; travel and adventure.

Answering machine: Air Element; communication problems; messages; bridging the gaps that keep people apart.

Arcade: Earth Element; playfulness or youthful outlooks; distraction or temptations; gambling with something.

Atom: Fire Element; energy; dramatic transformation; possible misuse of power.

Balloon: Air Element; lifting burdens and hope; inflated egos or ideas; possibly the need for grounding.

Bank: Earth Element; financial security; savings; frugality.

Bar: Earth/Water Elements; social interaction; secrets; relationships; troubles.

Bathroom scale: Earth Element; balance; weight loss; considering options.

Bomb: Earth Element; acting out of anger; destructive force that has no positive results.

Brick walls: Earth Element; overlooking the obvious; lack of attention; blocked progress.

Bubbles: Air/Water Elements; lightness; hope; uplifting occasions; joy.

Calculator: Earth Element; the conscious mind; financial matters under scrutiny.

Camera: Air/Fire Elements; surprise; special occasions; capturing the moment.

Car: Earth Element; movement; travel.

Chocolate: Fire Element; passion; sensual input; cravings; dietary changes; pleasurable pursuits.

Clock radio: Air Element; time; motivation; spiritual or mental awakenings.

Computer: Element varies by part; focus; memory; networking; communication.

Concrete: Earth Element; being very set in your ways; halted movement; strong foundations.

Condoms: Water Element; protection; wise choices; sexuality; modern morality.

Crockpot: Fire Element; slow change; harmonious mingling of different elements or people.

Doorbell: Air Element; good news; guests; hospitality.

Dryer: Fire/Air Elements; gentle warming of a situation; lightness or problems easing.

Electricity: Fire Element; power; channeling personal energy successfully.

False teeth: Water/Earth Elements; insecurity; falsehood; something hidden or misrepresented.

Filing cabinet: Earth Element; organize; cleaning; sorting of priorities.

Food processor: Water/Fire Elements; change of state; conforming to a situation.

Football: Earth Element; tackling a situation head on.

Gun: Fire Element; anger; lack of control; possible explosion in a heated situation.

Hairpiece: Earth Element; partial honesty; attention being directed toward superficial things.

Handcuffs: Earth Element; being bound to negative ideas or habits.

Laboratory: Fire Element; study; science; concentration; looking for solutions.

Lawn mower: Fire/Air Elements: cutting away old, useless concepts so new ones can grow.

Laser: Fire Element; accuracy; being on the cutting edge; clearly defined lines.

Microscope: Fire Element; close scrutiny; attention to detail; feeling small or insignificant.

Neon lights: Fire Element; being a bit of a primadonna or finding yourself starry-eyed.

Parachute: Air Element; bailing out of a situation carefully and gracefully; freedom or liberation.

Pizza: Various Elements; cycles; a slice of life or reality being served in a pleasant form; wheel of fortune.

Pollution: Element depends on area; awareness; cleansing; purification; reconnect with nature.

Remote control: Fire Element; power; possible manipulation; the need for regulation or supervision.

Revolving door: Water Element; cycles; the turning wheel; endings that lead to new beginnings.

Rocket: Fire Element; exploration; rapid growth; movement; universal awareness.

Satellite dish: Air Element; listening (or not) to good advice; receiving messages.

Synthesizer: All Elements; being able to blend, change and adapt to a new situation.

Telescope: Fire/Air Elements; being able to see things from a detached perspective; getting the big picture.

Television: Fire Element; distraction; diversion; the media.

Toothbrush: Water Element; hygiene; self-care; unsticking difficult situations.

Trash can: Earth Element; waste; prudence; keeping yourself free of psychic clutter.

Whirlpool: Water Element; blending; the need for relaxation; healing.

How else might you apply these types of interpretive values, as well as others you come up with? Try pondering them as dream symbols, adding them into visualizations, using them as spell components, or integrating them into rituals as tools/emblems. For example, use a paper airplane as part of a safe travel spell when you're traveling by plane, or place it in the Eastern Quarter of your ritual circle to represent the element of Air.

More in keeping with this chapter's theme, how about a modern key for omen observation? For example, if your answering machine sticks on a particular word or phrase, does this word or phrase have any meaning to a question or situation that's heavy on your heart? This approach doesn't advocate over-spiritualizing mundane matters, but it keeps you open and aware of your inner psychic as a potential ally in coping in today's busy world.

Chapter 7

A Witch's Kin

Then in mine there are bits of you, and in you there are bits of me.

—*Kuan Tao-Sheng*

As an organized belief system, Wicca is still very young, even though its premises are ancient. When the movement started taking real shape and definition in the 1970s, the average Witch was young and single. That is no longer the case. Witches in today's world have "grown up," moved out, gathered roommates, or entered into relationships, and many are rearing children and grandchildren in the Craft. This presents entirely new considerations for Witches about what's the best way to respectfully foster a magickal lifestyle inside the boundaries of a family-type unit and in children without manipulation.

The Nonmagickal Household

More and more young people are turning to Wicca as a way of reclaiming control of their lives. Many of these young adults do not live in homes where magick is understood or accepted. Other individuals who come into the Craft long after finding a mate may find themselves in similar situations—with a partner or housemates who are of different spiritual persuasions. This raises often-difficult questions about how open to be about one's choice of religion, and how to best present that information when the subject comes up.

To begin with, return to Chapter 2 where I talked about discussing the Craft. A great deal of the information there applies to a household setting, too. Don't expect a parent, lover, or housemate to understand your beliefs if you don't truly *live* them and if you don't explain things thoroughly when the opportunity presents itself. Likewise, don't expect that even after a long dissertation about the benefits of being a Witch that they'll change their minds. We still have a lot of prejudice to overcome and that requires time and patience.

Some Words for Teen Witches

I really don't recommend hiding your decision from your parents. The trust in that relationship is very fragile, and to gain your parents' respect you need to be honest with them. If you hide the truth and they find out from someone else, it's going to make coming out of your broom closet even harder.

Try giving them some good books to read so they're not frightened by the idea of their son or daughter being a Witch. Two good choices are *Drawing Down the Moon* by Margot Adler and *The Truth About Witchcraft* by Scott Cunningham. Trust me when I say that the news often sends even the most understanding, fair parents into a tizzy—because they don't know what Witchcraft today is really all about. Sit down and talk to them about what got you interested in this path and how it's affecting your life in positive ways. Points to stress in this conversation include:

- ◆ Wicca is an important part of your life that makes you happy, more aware, and a better overall person.

- ◆ Witchcraft helps you deal more effectively with all the problems and pressures teenagers face today.

- ◆ Witchcraft is not your way of "bucking the system"; it's a serious religion that advocates tolerance, respect, and peace.

- ◆ Wicca teaches you to be responsible toward yourself and the planet.

- ◆ You want them to be happy about your decision and hope they respect it. In turn, you promise not to allow your beliefs to step all over household traditions and ground rules.

Remember, you're still living at home, which means that you need to be sensitive toward what's important to the rest of your family. Don't expect everyone to start changing the way they celebrate Halloween just because you know it's New Year's, for example—and don't take this lack of change as an insult. It's not. It's just a different way of seeing things.

Creating a Bedroom or Closet Altar

In those instances when your family doesn't mind you having an altar, but perhaps not one that's out somewhere for everyone to see, consider setting up something special in your bedroom or closet. In both cases I don't recommend using candles without the express permission of your parents, and then use only those that are self-contained (for safety purposes).

To set up an altar you need only a small flat surface upon which to put Elemental symbols, special books/tools, and perhaps an image of the god/dess. I recommend a small incense burner (to represent Fire and Air) or a bowl of potpourri, some seasonal touches, such as pine cones in Winter, a shell or cup (to represent Water) or a ritual chalice, and a stone or living plant (to represent Earth). Change these decorations as you see fit and as inspiration moves you.

Go to this area when you pray, meditate, and study so it slowly absorbs positive magickal energy. There's kind of a neat symbolic element to having the altar in your closet. Opening the closet door opens the way for your magick to begin!

Studying Outside the Home

If you find your family is totally against your magickal path, you may want to constrain your studies to outside the home. Leave books and tools with a trusted friend. This way you can honor your parent's beliefs but still continue doing what's important to you elsewhere.

Even if you study outside the home, I don't advocate hiding your studies from them. Rather, find ways to earn your outside study or ritual time by doing extra chores or other thoughtful gestures. This shows your parents two very important things. First, it confirms that being a Witch isn't just a fad for you. Second, it reveals that even though you've chosen a different path, you still care about what your parents' thoughts and feelings. Most parents will respond positively to this kind of courtesy.

Mixed and Mingled Traditions

As you may have guessed, my family is pretty eclectic. I'm Wiccan, my husband practices a mixture of Shamanism and Buddhism, his family is Catholic, and mine is Lutheran. This makes for some interesting situations! For example, one time my sister called to ask if it was all right for my son to pray at her dinner table. She was concerned that I might consider it offensive to my beliefs. I had to stop and think about it for a moment, but then I realized that prayer is a good thing for children to learn and that

•

our children should be exposed to a variety of beliefs so they can make educated choices in the future. I told her to go ahead and let him join in the prayer.

On the home front, my husband's and my holidays don't always match, nor do our ways of honoring them. Over the years we've adjusted our lifestyle to make room for both traditions in and around the house. There's an altar upstairs with Buddha, and one downstairs dedicated to the god/dess. On certain new moons, my husband fasts. (I'm careful not to make his favorite meals those days!) This all sounds very simple, but it's the thoughtfulness that really counts here.

No matter who you're living with, talk to them about their beliefs and how you can respect those beliefs without giving up your own. Likewise, ask them to "make room" for your traditions too. For example, perhaps you can enjoy Yule on the 22nd your way, and they can celebrate Christmas on the 25th in their way. Around the house, give equal space to both approaches (many times you'll find the traditions overlap anyway).

As you're doing this, use it as an opportunity to compare and contrast traditions. Learn from one another! It will take a little time to come up with the right balance that makes everyone happy, but with honest effort it can happen. I truly believe you'll find the overall atmosphere of your living space improves from so doing.

The Magickal Family

I'm very fortunate in that my husband's path and mine work harmoniously together most of the time. This allows us to celebrate our beliefs privately, or as a unit. In the process of figuring these out for ourselves, we've come across some activities that everyone enjoyed. Perhaps you can make them a part of your own celebrations to make the world safer, more harmonious, and more magickal for everyone who lives in your home.

ACTIVITY: Making a Family Candle

For this activity you'll need a fair amount of candle drippings, preferably from candles you've used in magick for peace, joy, unity, and other similar qualities that you'd like to see manifest in your family. You'll also need a piece of wick two inches in length, something to weight it with, such as a button, a cleaned-out quart-sized milk carton, and a pencil that's long enough to go across the top of the milk carton. Also gather some finely powdered herbs that symbolize your wishes for the family (each person should choose one). Examples include lavender for joy, nutmeg for health, rose for love and luck, violet for peace, mint for protection, and sandalwood for spirituality.

Wait until the moon is full if possible. Secure one end of the wick to the pencil and the other end to the button, so that the button touches the bottom of the milk carton and the length in between is fairly taut. Put the wax cuttings into a nonaluminum pan over a low flame and gather everyone around the stove, which represents the warmth and the love of your household. Each person should take a turn stirring the wax clockwise and sprinkle in his or her herb, while verbalizing the wish it represents.

Let this mixture cool slightly before pouring it into the milk carton to set. Release the wax mixture from the mold by quickly dipping it in a sink full of hot water. Light this candle any time tensions or anger begin saturating your home, or for family spells and rituals.

ACTIVITY: Blessing Your Living Space

If you can get everyone together on a regular basis to perform spells that represent the entire family's needs, I think you'll naturally find the activity improves unity and family ties. One spell in particular that's nice to do at least once a year is a house blessing. We spend at least 10 hours of every day in our living spaces. Regular blessings keep these spaces saturated with positive magickal energy, which naturally fosters the safety and well-being of your family and everyone who visits you.

For this spell you need a fire-safe container with sand or dirt and some self-lighting charcoal. You also need a pinch or two of purifying/protective powdered incense blend (sandalwood, frankincense, and myrrh is one option) and a feather or hand-held fan. Have everyone gather in a central room (the family room and dining room are good choices).

Light the incense. Hold hands and visualize your love pouring into the smoke as a white light. Add an incantation such as this:

"BE FILLED WITH OUR LOVE AND SACRED POWER,
BLESS OUR HOME THIS MAGICKAL HOUR!"

Now move clockwise around the house, having each person take a turn dispersing the incense into a room with the feather or fan. Repeat the incantation in each room. Afterward, spend some family time together to do something fun. The pleasure you find in your kinship augments the magick.

ACTIVITY: Food Sorcery

While the routines of our daily lives might inspire more takeout food than home cooking, the modern Witch recognizes the benefit of stirring positive energy into any meal (even those that come from a box). Better still, if you have family recipes, adding a magickal dimension to them only increases the special feeling they transport through smells and flavors.

Making kitchen magick a family activity isn't difficult. Your children or housemates can read the directions aloud, measure ingredients, or stir a pot. Maybe one or two of them can hum a favorite magickal song or chant while you work. Encourage everyone's participation, however, so that in this case many hands make the magick! The blending of personal energies into the meal helps internalize harmony and unity when you eat the food.

Don't forget to get a little creative! Here are few of the ideas my family has come up with to make food magick a lot of fun:

- Add a bit of pink food coloring to a loving family cake and bake it in a heart-shaped tin.

- Cut a dollar sign in the top of homemade (or even frozen) prosperity bread dough so the money rises with the loaf. Add a pinch of blessed dill to support the spell.

- Find cookie cutters in the shapes of trees to make Earth Day munchies.

- Make gingerbread people and decorate them to look like family members so each person internalizes the energy and zest of ginger. This is an alternative poppet!

- Slice cheese-flavored hot dogs, pattern them like a smile, and serve them on a platter when someone is sad (I guarantee a little laugh).

Creating Rituals

Ritual offers a way for us to come together and celebrate our ties and our love. To create family rituals, however, you have to consider three things: your living space, the ages and aptitudes of your housemates, and the ritual's theme. This trinity creates a strong foundation upon which to build our ritual: The structure of that space determines how much action and/or decoration we can have, house members' ages/aptitudes determine much of the body of the ritual (especially words), and the theme rounds out the rest.

While you can certainly turn to books of ritual for guidelines or ideas, such as my book, *Wiccan Basic Rituals and Ceremonies*, I strongly suggest trying to assemble at least one family ritual that you work with annually. The process encourages every member of your household to consider what that ritual means to him or her individually, as well as to the entire family unit. Consequently, the meaningfulness and power generated are bound to improve.

Most rituals follow a basic pattern that you can use in creating your own. That pattern is:

- ♦ **Create sacred space:** This should help the whole family focus on magick rather than mundane matters.

- ♦ **An opening:** Such as a prayer, the lighting of candles, holding hands, or other similar activities.

- ♦ **A body:** This is where the theme of the ritual finds expression. The body of a ritual might include spells, meditations, music, theatrical performance, charm creation, and/or dancing to help highlight the theme and build power.

- ♦ **An apex:** This is where the energy created by the ritual gets directed toward its goal.

- ♦ **An offering or libation (liquid offering)** to your family's preferred vision of the god or goddess.

- ♦ **A declaration:** This statement of purpose helps bring everyone back down to Earth to focus on the closing.

- ♦ **A closing:** This dismisses the Quarters/Guardians or Watchtowers and often includes final thoughts or prayers.

Within this basic structure I think you'll find there's plenty of leeway to integrate your family's needs, vision, and traditions as desired. When you're done, try the ritual and make notes of how it all worked out in the family Book of Shadows.

<u>ACTIVITY: A Family Book of Shadows</u>

Because Wicca is still young, we don't have a lot of long-lived traditions upon which to depend. Yes, there are those from the ancient past, but what the ancients did and what constitutes Witchery today are often two very different things. So, it's really up to us to create traditions for ourselves and future generations. One way of doing just that is by recording the spells, charms, meditations, rituals, and other magickal methods that your family (or family members) create in a family Book of Shadows.

You can accomplish this in any number of ways. Buy a blank diary, use a three-ring binder, type it on the computer, or get really fancy and make homemade paper and have the book bound. Whatever your choice, this should be a group effort. Younger children can color borders for the book, while adult members can actually work on writing entries in a format that's understandable and well-organized.

As the years move forward, make sure this book gets passed on to other family members who are interested in magick and in continuing the tradition your family has created together. In time, this will become a treasured keepsake that blesses future generations with your magick and your vision for their world!

Children and the Craft

Many modern Witches struggle with how to raise children, feeling that they should be free to choose their own spiritual path. But until they are mature enough, children need some type of spiritual guidelines to round out the growing process. I believe there are ways of accomplishing this without overstepping the bounds of free will or good parenting. Specifically, we can create various learning activities that teach our children to honor the Earth, be good people, celebrate the seasons, and also celebrate their individuality. At the same time we can begin to arm them against the difficulties they will face in the future.

I came to this conclusion with Karl, my first child, who had an uncanny knack for seeing spirits. He was in constant contact with my deceased father. The situation was more than just a little hard to explain to outsiders! I told my son that his grandfather was like a guardian angel, staying close by to keep an eye on him. This seemed to satisfy everyone—not just my son. In this way I didn't have to discourage my son's ability, and at the same time I gave him and others around us a "user-friendly" way of interpreting the experience.

Another example came to me by way of a rainy camping weekend. Karl, then 7, was miserable about the weather. I asked him how he would make the rain go away if he was able. He looked around and walked over to a standing torch without a second thought. He blew on the smoke coming from the torch so it moved in the opposite direction. Within an hour the sky cleared!

When Karl asked me why this worked, I gently explained that the Great Spirit abides in all things, including the Wind. By blowing on the torch, it was a way of expressing his prayer to the Sacred without using words, and the prayer was answered. My explanation allowed for a generic religious appeal, in case he ever recounted the story to anyone, but still planted powerful magickal seeds in him, the sprouts from which are still growing.

Older children face harder questions because of peer pressure. They need to learn how to handle jibes from schoolmates about "Mom the Witch," if your family is openly Wiccan. Even if you're not, you (and they) are bound to come across someone who asks what church you go to—and other very awkward questions for preteens and teens. The best answer to give your children to many such questions is that your family treats religion as a private matter and you'd rather not talk about it. A bit of a cop out, I admit, but its much easier for kids to handle than trying to explain the truth (at least until the world is a little more accepting of alternative paths).

Under no circumstances, however, do I recommend hiding your faith from your children. Trust is so fragile in the parent-child relationship, and personal or family beliefs are much too important to sweep under the rug. The greatest gifts you can give your children are an honest awareness of what you believe and insights into what others believe. These gifts will help your children be tolerant from a young age. Whether or not they embrace magick in the future doesn't matter half as much as providing them with the knowledge and wisdom to make the right choice.

If they do choose a magickal path, you can consider several ways of celebrating and honoring that choice. (Although there is no minimum age for initiation into the Craft, I recommend 18.) Here are some ideas to consider:

♦ Have the child help design his or her own initiation ritual, or a ritual in which you welcome him or her as a fully responsible magickal member of the family.

♦ Help the child find/make magickal tools, such as wands and tarot cards. As you gather each tool, take the opportunity to explain its proper use and care.

♦ Encourage some kind of weekly magickal study and practice, be it designing a spell, reading a book, or talking over questions with you and other respected members of the community.

♦ Encourage some kind of daily meditation. Especially in the teen years, learning to focus is a great talent that helps with schoolwork as well as magick.

♦ Help the child build a magickal library filled with books that you know have good information, and that he or she can refer to often for insights. (See the Appendix for possibilities to get you started.)

♦ Start doing seasonal crafts for decorating the family altar (or even that of your larger circles). Any art that the child excels in will tap his or her creative well and express magickal ideas in tangible forms.

♦ Most importantly, let the child tackle magick at his or her own pace (not yours). I have often found that children of Wiccan families are wise beyond their years and end up teaching *us!*

Special Activities for Children

Children are naturally receptive to spiritual energy. To enrich their lives with simple spiritually centered activities, try some of these.

ACTIVITY: Ritual Plays

Kids love to pretend and play make-believe. Consider a theatrical production in which your children are both the stars of the show and active participants in creating the whole play, including the script and props. Because ritual plays are artistic expressions, they give you a lot of freedom in how you portray the theme of the ritual in which this mini-play occurs (as part of the ritual's body). Here are some examples:

- ◆ Spring rituals: Design a play in which the kids get to portray the Earth's reawakening. One child might be a tree whose sap begins to fill the branches, another might be a seed getting warmed by the new sun, and so forth.

- ◆ Moon rituals: Have the children create a dance that inspires the moon to wax or wane (or perhaps mimics it). They can make silver-toned costumes with lots of glitter so that by the light of the ritual candles or fires they look like moving moons!

- ◆ Wish rituals: Create a play in which the wish spell actually gets cast, then the remainder of the play acts out its manifestation. This is a terrific way to introduce your children to sympathetic/imitative magick.

I think you'll find the whole process of putting together ritual plays is really fun for the kids—and it gives you a terrific opportunity to answer their questions about magick. The quality time you're spending together shouldn't be overlooked either.

ACTIVITY: Making a Sleepy Bear

This is a great item to make for younger kids, because young children are prone to night fears and bad dreams. To make the magick sleepy bear who helps keep monsters far, far away you'll need two pieces of fake fur about 2-x-2 in size, some cotton batting, and a sachet filled with balsam needles, rose petals, lavender, and mint. From the two fabric pieces cut two bear-like outlines that are exactly the same size. If your child is old enough to help with any step of this process, encourage him or her to do so. It makes a child feel more in control of his or her fears.

Next, put the furry side of the fabric patterns together and sew all but a few inches in the head. Turn this shape inside out and stuff it up to the belly with cotton batting to fill out the legs. Right around the bear's belly button area, put the herbal sachet so it's well wrapped with bunting (this keeps the bear soft). Continue adding bunting now until the bear is filled, then sew up the last edge repeating an incantation such as:

"GOOD THOUGHTS AND HAPPY DREAMS,
HELD WITHIN THIS TEDDY BEAR'S SEAMS!"

Now you can have the child help you decorate the bear by picking out button eyes (or drawing them on with markers), and maybe dressing it in doll clothes. Put this in or near the child's bed each night.

For older children, you might want to think about helping them design their own bedtime blessing instead (akin to a nightly prayer) that wraps them in protection and good energy.

Giving Old Favorites a Magickal Twist

In thinking back to my youth, I realize that there was a lot of magickal potential in many of the games I loved. For example, how about hopscotching your way toward a goal? Have children name the stone after their wishes or needs, then jump to create energy that supports the spell. Other ideas along these lines include:

♦ **Jump rope incantations:** Make up various magickal rhymes that indicate a child's needs or wishes and help him or her recite these when jumping rope. As with hopscotch, the jumping creates energy that helps with manifestation, and the verbal element fills the air around the child with sympathetic vibrations.

♦ **Skipping stone divination:** Go to a pond or stream and teach your child how to skip stones. To learn the answer to a specific question, he or she can concentrate on that question before tossing the stone. If it doesn't skip, but sinks, it's a definite no. The farther the stone goes, the more positive the sign, especially if it skips an even number of times.

♦ **Hula-hoop energy:** As this toy spins in circles you can use the energy created to augment various types of magick. Clockwise spinning is positive and draws things into a child's life; counterclockwise spinning helps with banishing or diminishing magick. The child simply needs to keep a strong mental image of the goal at hand while he or she plays.

♦ **Magickal Scrabble or word jumbles:** Try playing various word games using all magickal terms. It's a great way to introduce various ideas to your children. Word jumbles in particular symbolically help them unravel the deeper meaning of the jumbled word.

♦ **Coloring happy:** Coloring activities can be used for a wide variety of magickal goals. For example, when a child is sad give him or her an outline of an image that looks a bit like him or her to color happy. Have the child use bright, life-affirming colors, such as red (although this varies from person to person), for this particular goal. The colors and the act of coloring gives the magick a visual form upon which a child can easily focus. Change the activity in both imagery and colors to mirror the needs at hand.

♦ **Puzzle empowerment:** When your child is having trouble understanding something or bringing a particular type of energy into his or her life, try this activity. Create a collage out of cardboard and magazine clippings that represents a positive outcome for whatever issue is at hand. Cut the collage up like a puzzle and let him or her assemble it again and again.

As the child puts the puzzle pieces together, he or she is also symbolically drawing that energy to himself or herself.

For more ideas along these lines, I suggest you look at toys and games that have lots of hands-on appeal and visual stimuli to keep a child's interest. You'll probably find a few other adaptable playthings that your child already likes around the house.

Opening the Lines of Communication

Many children don't know how to approach their parents about problems. Communication difficulties are bountiful in even the best magickal home because of all the distractions we have around us. A talking stick helps solve at least part of this problem because it becomes a signal between you and your child that says, "I need to talk now."

A talking stick can be made out of anything. I personally like to use long, fallen branches that can double as hiking staffs or ritual wands. Your child should be encouraged to decorate this in any way that seems suited to its use. For example, Air best helps with matters of communication so he or she might want to add some feathers or other Air symbols to the talking stick.

Bless the stick with your child in a manner that feels right, perhaps with a prayer or incantation. Then tell him or her that whenever they want your attention, all he or she has to do is simply leave the talking stick in a prescribed location. As soon as you see it, go to your child and find out what's up!

Commemorating the Seasons

Every season has a special energy and lessons to teach us. Come Spring, focus on Wind spells (maybe using kites), seed spells (for personal growth and change), and wish magick. Summer is well-suited to flowering spells (so that magick blossoms) and various types of sun magick. Fall might be the time to discuss Water-related spells and to start doing more pantry magick as a way of conserving one's resources and energies for the Winter. And Winter is for Earth-magick and indoor studies. It's also a fun season for playing with ice and snow spells if you live in a four-season environment.

As you design these activities make sure you transfer the most successful and enjoyable ones to your family Book of Shadows to use again in the years ahead. This way you begin creating a tradition that sings the song of your family's soul, and will continue to do so for many years to come.

◆ ◆ ◆

You accomplish a great deal by participating in these activities with your children. First, you help them realize they're an important part of the magickal family unit. Second, you begin making them aware of nature—this planet's gentle teacher and a great mirror of the Sacred Planet. Third, you keep the child's spiritual nature from drying up or becoming hardened (as many of us experienced before we found Witchery). Fourth, you plant in them the awareness that the whole world has magickal potential (including them) if they but look at it differently.

Finally, so many of our children have lost a sense of uniqueness—of feeling important and wanted. These activities and similar ones nip that negativity in the bud. Any child involved in positive spiritual exercises guided by loving hands will quickly see that he or she is a special, magickal being whose energy is not only wanted, but needed, in this world.

Chapter 8

All in a Day's Magick

I took the road less traveled by, and that has made all the difference.

—Robert Frost

From space, the Earth quietly turns on its axis against a calm backdrop of stars. What happens on this planet between daybreak and dusk, however, is anything but calm and serene! This hectic pace presses us ever onward, collectively and individually, leaving many people feeling trapped by the momentum of daily responsibilities.

On many mornings the closest I come to having a religious experience is a cup of coffee. As I sit at the table, trying to get inspired to move to the computer and begin writing, I know that there must be a better way—not for just me, but for all of today's Witches. We all need to find ways to transform the mundane into something magickal, which has really been the purpose of this entire book.

For those reading this who find themselves nodding a vehement yes, understanding of what I speak, this chapter will help you as it helped me. This is my answer for finding ways to cope with daily reality in down-to-earth, magickal ways. I realize your daily routines will vary from mine, so what I've tried to do here is compile some common, everyday experiences to which a little magick can be added with the least amount of fuss. This will allow you to move your magick out of a passive role and into an active, life-affirming one any moment of any day, by yourself or with those you love.

Magick Throughout the Day

In the years ahead, I believe being adaptable is going to become even more essential to people of all faiths. We have a lot of challenges facing us, challenges for which our beliefs can offer perspectives and proactive alternatives. But before we can think too much about tomorrow, we have to get today under control!

I don't know about you, but I push the snooze button one too many times, jump out of bed, and then rush around the house. For those with jobs outside your home, this means getting dressed, facing traffic, going to work, rushing back home, preparing dinner, grabbing the newspaper, watching the news, and maybe taking an hour to talk to their spouses/mates before it's time to go to bed and start over again. Does this sound familiar?

Here are some ways you can make minor changes in your daily schedule that bring magick back to the forefront of your life.

Morning Devotional

At 6 a.m. in my home, the children are starting to stir, the dog wants to go out, and the cats are meowing for food. I can do one of two things: Jump up and get started, or pause for a moment of calm reflection. Whenever possible, I choose the latter.

Before you get out of bed, take a moment to breathe deeply, stretch, and wake up all your senses. This is a good way to fill your spiritual gas tank before heading into a busy day. Next, I recommend going to your altar (or even a dresser) and lighting a candle by way of welcoming the Sacred into your world. Say hello to your vision of the god/dess and ask for whatever you need to make that day as magickally and personally fulfilling as possible. While these two things sound very simple, I can tell you that they set a totally different tone for your entire day. When I don't follow this morning ritual, I find that the rhythm and mood of the day often feels off, out of kilter, and just plain drab. Yet, it takes but moments to accomplish these two tasks, and shine the light of magick into my daily world.

Preparation Affirmations

While you're standing in front of the mirror in the morning to brush your teeth, wash, and/or shave, why not make the most of that time? Who says these things can't help bring you more spiritual-mindedness? Not me!

For example, while you're washing your face, affirm your best attributes out loud to yourself. Say with confidence, "I am worthwhile" or "I am a special, magickal being." This is not an exercise in ego, but a way of acknowledging and supporting those things in yourself that you either (a) don't give yourself enough credit for, or (b) want to keep activated as coping mechanisms. In both cases, the purpose is to continue growing, learning, and being the best person you can be on all levels. These affirmations fill the air with the right vibrations to help with that goal.

But what about brushing your teeth, say you? How can I do anything positive with that time? Well, how about naming stubborn bits of food after sticky situations in your life. Then the energy you put toward brushing and flossing can help loosen those circumstances up too!

ACTIVITY: Dancing with Dawn

Once a month, set your alarm clock for sunrise. Get up and go somewhere quiet where you can look out a window and see the first golden rays of dawn peek across the horizon. Settle your mind and heart and listen closely to the world around you. Watch in silence as the Earth is reborn, and with it your hope.

As the orange-pink light of a new day meets you, let it saturate your being. Breathe this energy into yourself as if it were air, filling each cell and muscle with vitality, strength, and renewal. As you feel this power building (often noticeable by increased body warmth), stand and dance with the sunlight. Reach your arms out to embrace the beams, and feel the sun reach back! Thank the Sacred Powers for a new day of magick. Thank the Earth for her generosity.

Waltz and celebrate this moment, savoring it until you need to go get ready for your day. When you leave this place, take a moment to reflect on it in your magickal journal or share it with a friend. I suspect you'll find you carry more joy in your heart all day long, and even in the weeks ahead until you dance with the dawn once more.

By the way, you can change the timing of this activity to suit other personal needs. For example, dance with the noon-time sun to refill the inner energy wells. Dance with the dusk when something is ending, prance with the moonlight to inspire your intuitive self, and frolic with the stars at midnight to improve your awareness of the astral world.

Putting on the Magick

In some ways getting dressed in the morning is like preparing for a role in a play. Whether or not we enjoy this part, it's one we have to play out. By using your dressing time as a form of meditation, you can begin to ease some of the discomfort you may feel in taking on particular daily roles, or help improve your performance in those roles (if not both).

Begin by laying out your clothes on a bed or chair. Name each piece of clothing after a particular attribute you need to work effectively that day. For example, if you happen to be a manager you might name your pants "authority" and your tie "respectability." As you put on that garment, visualize yourself going through your day in the most positive, empowered way you can imagine. Continue in this manner until you have literally put on the visage and energy of everything necessary for this play called life.

I do not recommend this exercise for when you're meeting dates, friends, or loved ones, because you want to be yourself with these people. When you get home, don't forget to remove the workaday world in much the same way as you donned it. With each piece of clothing removed, let your burdens drop to the floor. Try not to pick these up immediately, as that symbolically accepts back the tensions and other energies from your day.

Shake yourself out and stretch again as you did first thing in the morning (this creates a positive cycle that ends the way it began). Put on something comfortable and leave that "other you" aside until you need him or her again.

On-the-Road Relaxation

I got this idea from a friend who uses her morning commute to listen to books on tape. It occurred to me that our hours in the car and on the bus, subway, or airplane represent a great chance to participate in any number of magickally centered activities. Practice your breathing exercises, put on your favorite witchy music or chants (or sing them yourself), or if you can find Wiccan books on tape, play those. Use this time to generate more good vibrations within and without to make your whole day flow more easily.

Lunch-Break Blessings

You have 30 or 60 minutes to yourself in the middle of the day, so if there's a spell you've been meaning to write, some magickal research you've wanted to do, or a visualization you'd like to try, pack it as part of your lunch! I don't think anyone will wonder about you writing in a notebook or just sitting quietly while you nibble, and this reclaims some valuable moments to focus yourself back toward spiritual matters.

End-of-Day Stress Reduction

The fast pace of most people's lives tends to produce stress, no matter what we might wish. Stress and anxiety are very anti-magick. They act as a huge stopper that holds back the well of the inner Witch. Worse, this tension begins to saturate the sacred space of home and undo the good energy you've placed therein. So, finding effective ways to de-stress will improve your Witchery and your daily life a lot. Here are some ideas for you to try and see what helps the most:

Physical Exercise

What's great about a long walk, isometrics, stretching, toe touches, yoga, aerobics, and/or other forms of exercise is that they not only rejuvenate your body and improve circulation, but they also help burn off a lot of excess tension. Consult with your physician to discover what forms of exercise are right for you, and consider which of these fit into your schedule with the least amount of fuss. And don't forget to use this time creatively by adding chanting, visualization, and good magickal music.

Breathing and Auric Balance

When you get home at night, try to set aside about 10 minutes for yourself before you start your evening routine. Go somewhere private and shake out every part of your body. Release the tension in your muscles, and breathe very deeply and evenly.

Pay particular attention to your shoulders—if they're hunched low, you're not done until they're resting at a normal level.

Next, take the palms of your hands and turn them toward yourself. Do a quick auric self-check. Are there any areas of your body where the energy field seems really odd, itchy, or extended? If so, focus your attention on smoothing those areas out so they're harmonious with the rest of your aura. If there's someone in your family with auric sensitivity, you might even ask for his or her help with this.

It's impossible for our minds or bodies to work at peak efficiency when our aura is out of kilter. This rule of "as without, so within" works on a very intimate level. The byproducts of this breathing activity are more than worthwhile. They include improved resistance to sickness and a greater sense of symmetry to take with you into your daily life.

Private Time

In the ebb and flow of things, we often neglect to give ourselves enough private time. In these quiet moments of the soul we get to sort things out and really listen to the voice of Spirit—rather than the noise that constantly surrounds.

One thing I do is to take a long, luxurious bath or shower once a week. I ask my husband to watch the kids while I have a few minutes of peace. It's amazing how much just 10 minutes change my entire demeanor. Try to find something similar to do for yourself. Maybe take a walk or read a few pages of a good book. Whatever you do, really savor it, so you can take that energy back with you as a coping mechanism, until the next opportunity you get to steal some private time!

Solo Social Time

When you live with others, it's easy to shape your reality according to that unit. This isn't always healthy; it can actually increase your stress levels because of other people's expectations. Sometimes we need a break to define ourselves outside that setting, to extend the facets of our personality and relieve ourselves from the pressures of those relationships if but for a few hours.

Rather than being alone, however, this time get together with a group of people. It can be a study group or a group of total strangers, but make it a social setting where you can talk and interact. Gather some new ideas or fresh perspectives, and laugh a lot. I promise you'll feel better afterward.

Dreamtime Magick

The end of another day arrives, but not all of us sleep soundly. Any Witch will tell you that magick always works more effectively when you're well-rested. And, thanks to our ancestors, we have a lot of magickal options for encouraging a restful night's sleep, and perhaps even some visionary dreams! Here are some to try:

Meditation/Visualization

This often helps you relax enough to drift effortlessly into sleep. Envision places where you feel peaceful and welcome.

Herb Teas

Try drinking catnip, valerian, chamomile, or mint tea before bed. Bless your herbs so the hot water releases the natural magick within!

Dream Pillows

Place a little sachet filled with mint, rosemary, lavender, hops, marigold petals, and rose petals into the center of any pillow. (The size of the pillow—and the desired scent—will determine the quantity of herbs you use.) Make sure the bundle is well-padded (a lumpy pillow won't make for a sound sleep).

Dream Catchers

Coming to us from Native American traditions, a dream catcher is hung over one's bed to filter out nightmares. Usually they're made from grapevines with some type of spider-web center that's decorated with feathers and crystals. These are readily available at many gift shops today, but find one whose stones and other decorations really appeal to your higher senses to experience the best results.

ACTIVITY: Taking a Moon Bath

Out beneath the moonlight, in the shadow of a star, great Witchery can be born. It was once said that Witches gained their power from the moon. Now you'll be using this idea to revitalize your intuitive, magickal self.

Wait until the moon is waxing or full. These two cycles symbolize growth, fertility, prosperity, psychism, and being able to "go with the flow." Go somewhere that you can bask in this moon's light. (A window will work, but outdoors is better.) Close your eyes and welcome the light of the Goddess, the timeless mother who embodies the energy of imagination and wholeness. Let that silvery light fill you, hold you, and heal you. Even as you danced with the dawn, now frolic under the moon and enrich your existence with fulfilling magick.

Magick for Everyday Situations

Besides these points in your day, there are a lot of other situations or needs that arise regularly in our lives to which one might want to apply some creative Witchery. Here are some ideas on how to handle some of those circumstances with a unique magickal flair:

Job Hunting

Go through the newspaper and clip out all the ads that seem like good leads. Please be realistic considering your training and experience. Write down the information about these listings on a separate sheet of paper that you can refer back to later. This way, you can take the clippings themselves to your altar.

Next, light a pinch or two of prosperity incense (perhaps basil and cinnamon) and burn the clippings with it. This releases your wishes and the possibilities to the winds and the Sacred. Visualize the smoke reaching out from you toward the various companies represented, bearing your magick with it. Keep the ashes from this as a portable charm to take to interviews.

Upon returning from those interviews, put the business cards you've collected under your telephone. This acts as a type of sympathetic magick to encourage a call from the right company. Continue this process until the best offer comes along.

Note, however, that our blessings sometimes come in odd packaging. Always weigh each job offer against your inner voice. For example, a company may offer you more money, but if the job being offered isn't as secure or fulfilling, it's not the best option. If you're looking for longevity or satisfaction, it might be best to take a little less salary with another firm where you feel you'll be happy for a long time.

Manifesting Wishes

We have what I call a wishing bowl in our home. Every morning before I leave the house for any reason, I light a candle, drop some spare change into the bowl, make a wish, and then blow out the candle. When the jar is full, I give the coins to a good cause as a way of thanks for the wishes that the universe has fulfilled.

To make your own wishing bowl, take a fish-style bowl and affix a white candle (spiritually generic for any need/goal) to the middle of the bottom with a drop of wax. Scatter a handful or so of pine needles around the candle for productive energy, lavender flowers for wish magick, and an elder leaf for good luck. Put this in a window to receive warm sunlight (releasing the fragrance of the herbs) and moonlight (to emphasize magick).

Achieving Goals

For this spell, you're going to first need to make a special anointing oil consisting of a drop or two each of ginger for success, sage for fulfillment, thyme for courage, and cinnamon for energy. Steep the herbs in warm oil during a full moon. Note that this oil need not be overly fragrant, but adding some essential oil to the blend can act like aromatherapy that will support your spell.

Strain the oil and put it in a bottle that's labeled with a list of your goals. Each time you begin working on one of those ambitions, dab a chakra whose energies will most help you with the oil. For example, if your goal is improving your relationship with a significant other, you'd dab your heart chakra.

If you wish, you can add an incantation at this point, but it's more important that you fully focus on your goal. Envision the chakra opening up and releasing the necessary vibrations into your aura. You can then go about your tasks confidently.

Feeling Attractive

Appearances mean a lot in the workaday world, even if they shouldn't. Consequently, it's common for people to want to feel desirable or attractive. If you find yourself in this position, you might want to return to Chapter 1 and try some of the activities there. Alternatively, try this bit of glamoury.

Glamoury is a type of metaphysical illusion that supports self-images in times of need. Additionally, as the name implies, it provides a unique spiritual "glamour" to your aura that makes you more noticeable. Before you start, look over this list of color symbolism and decide what best suits your situation:

- ♦ **Red:** Lots of passion and physical energy.
- ♦ **Orange:** Friendly and warm, like an autumn night's fire.
- ♦ **Yellow:** Very creative, communicative, and insightful.

- **Blue:** Calm and happy.
- **Green:** Productive, fertile energy
- **Purple:** Spiritual orientation; leadership qualities.
- **White:** Safety or purity.
- **Pink:** When you need to literally be "in the pink."
- **Black:** A message that says "keep your distance."

Once you've chosen the color that, to you, best represents your goal, get comfortable and start meditating. Shake off any stress and focus your mind wholly on your desire to pour specific energies into your aura.

Visualize colored light pouring down from overhead like a waterfall. This light shimmers, and its dominant color fills the auric envelope of your body from your feet up. As it does, you'll feel a warmth or tingling sensation.

Continue the visualization until the colored light specks surround you, twirling clockwise with power throughout your auric field (think of fairy dust with an attitude). This energy will stay in place until you release it expressing your desires, intentions, or goals without words.

By the way, for those of you interested in shamanic magick, working with glamoury is an excellent primer for shape shifting.

Breaking Habits

Witches are people, too. (Boy, I'd like that on a bumper sticker!) We have faults to overcome just like everyone else. But there's no reason we can't use magick to help this process along!

I find this spell very helpful when I discover the need to make personal changes that seem overwhelming or unmanageable. Begin with a small flammable object that represents the habit or negative thought-form you wish to overcome. Place this on a fire source with a pinch or two of herbs that represent change and growth (perhaps clove, cinnamon, and myrrh). As you put this token to the fire, visualize yourself sitting in the midst of the flames with it, the fire neatly burning away any unwanted, oppressive energies.

As the fire cleanses these things, inhale the aromas of the herbs to internalize the positive energy. Allow your visualization to continue developing. See your shape changing. You are becoming the image of a phoenix, who always rises from the ashes more beautiful and better than ever before. With this image firm in your mind, take that energy into the challenge or situation at hand. Use this as a driving force to make concrete, tangible efforts so the magick can work through and for you.

Finding Lost Items

There's nothing more frustrating than misplacing something (or having a deva misplace it for you!). I've used this activity successfully to find lost items, especially when I don't have a lot of time to hunt around. To try it yourself you'll need a rubber band that you've cut (so that it's more like an expandable piece of string), a piece of paper with an image or the name of the item on it, and a piece of chewed bubble gum. Attach the gum to one end of the rubber band.

Next, adhere the paper to the rubber band at the same end as the bubble gum. Hold the loose end in your hand. Think about the lost item. Repeat the phrase "return to me" 13 times, then tug on the rubber band. If it breaks, you may not be able to retrieve your possession. If the end with the paper attached springs into your hand, the object will find its way home soon (or you'll remember where you put it). If it takes several tugs to free the rubber band, it's going to take some real hunting to find this object so wait until you have more time. The number of tugs may portend the number of days or hours the search will take.

Overcoming Technical Glitches

Witches are surrounded by technology, much of which can be a great helpmate to daily life and our magick. But when that technology breaks down, it drains pocketbooks and wastes a lot of valuable personal time. This is the spell that I use to avoid such situations. It helps keep my favorite gadgets working at peak efficiency.

The main component for this spell is a bay leaf, placed near the gadget in question. If small bits of herb would damage that item, cover the bay leaf with some type of protective sheath, such as a piece of waxed paper that has been ironed shut.

Put your hands palm down over the bay leaf. Visualize a white, protective light pouring into it and repeat this incantation three times:

"OF BUGS BE FREE, HEAR WHAT I SAY.

KEEP ALL GLITCHES AWAY

FROM WHERE I PLACE THIS DAY!"

From an herbal viewpoint, bay leaves are known to deter bug infestation. We're applying this symbolism on an astral level by putting the empowered bay leaf near or under machinery!

Quieting Irritating People

We don't have to sit back and nonchalantly take all the ill-will the world dishes out. But we *do* need to get a little creative with our magick so as to not manipulate or intentionally harm another—in this case those who have an uncanny ability to get under our skin.

Here's one spell that I really like, and it falls neatly into the nonmanipulative category. You'll need a small, hand-held mirror, a pinch of banishing herbs, such as powdered garlic, mixed with glue, and a piece of paper upon which the person's name is written. Glue this paper face down on the mirror. This achieves two things. They then have to face themselves and their actions honestly, and any negativity they send out will reflect right back onto them.

During the gluing process you might want to add a specific incantation that indicates the problematic area. Using gossip as an illustration you might say:

"WHEN YOU SPEAK, LET ONLY TRUTH BE HEARD.

LIES WILL WITHER IN YOUR WORDS."

Again, this incantation is designed to affect someone who is purposefully spreading half-truths. The results can be interesting. Sometimes a person will begin to repeat some gossip and will stutter or completely lose his or her train of thought. This certainly isn't harmful to the individual, but it (hopefully) makes him or her more aware of personal actions/culpability.

Healing Sickness

Witches throughout the ages have been adept healers, tending to the needs of their families and entire communities. Today's Witches want to reclaim this heritage, but it's not always easy in a world where metaphysical healing is often looked upon as questionable. Even so, tending our bodies means taking care of them on an auric/astral level. Based on the idea of "as without, so within," if our spiritual energy is out of sync, our bodies suffer to varying degrees.

Thanks to the New Age movement, some ancient holistic practices have returned to us, including herbalism, aromatherapy, bio-feedback, reiki, and massage. Which of these (if any) a Witch chooses to practice is purely personal, but most of them require professional assistance. Here are several hints for Witches who want to metaphysically attend to health matters without spending a fortune:

♦ **Set up a routine of spiritual cleansing for yourself and your sacred space of home.** We carry around a lot of negativity from one day to the next. Cleansing banishes excess tension, anger, frustration, and worry, which, in turn, improves overall well-being, not to mention magickal flow. Try smudging your aura and home with sage or cedar smoke, bathe yourself and wash your floors in lemon water, visualizing everything filled with sparkling white light, or other similar approaches from your personal tradition.

♦ **Meditate before you go to bed at night.** Breathe deeply and evenly to reconnect with your spiritual nature. Let this energy wrap you in comfort and warmth. You'll find that you sleep more peacefully, which refreshes your body and provides more power with which to sustain wellness.

♦ **Comb your aura regularly using incense or a feather.** Pay particular attention to areas that are out of balance, rough, or seemingly void. These are the areas that house sickness or stress. Combing your aura into balance helps the body's natural resistance tackle these regions more effectively.

♦ **Try a knot spell.** This is to bind a specific malady. To be most effective use yarn or rope in a color that represents banishing (such as black or a very dark blue). Lay this over the area where the problem resides and visualize the robe absorbing the negative energy. Tie the robe tightly saying:

"I BIND _____ WITHIN STRING, [fill in the blank with the area where the problem resides]
FROM THIS DAY ON ONLY WELLNESS BRING!"

Ritually burn or bury the token afterwards so the negative energy disappears.

♦ **Make a healing poppet.** Take two items of clothing that you no longer need and cut out the rough image of a person in them. Stitch all but the head of this poppet together, with their right sides inward. Stuff it with herbs such as chamomile, sage, cedar, and mint, which are known for their healing properties. As you stitch up the last side repeat an incantation such as this:

"Good health to me, I'm a healing witch,
let magick be sown in every stitch!"

Keep the poppet near you so it fills the air around you with healthful energies. Alternatively, ritually burn or bury the doll to banish the sickness it represents.

♦ **Wash it away.** Take a plain rock and some water colors. Paint the rock with an image that represents your problem. Hold the rock under running water (a stream is best, but a faucet works, too) and purposefully rub away the image on the stone. Repeat this incantation as you wash:

"Away, away, all sickness away.
I will be healthy beginning today!"

Carry the stone as a health amulet.

♦ **Make a healthful potion.** Begin with a base of 1 cup each orange and apple juice in a blender. Add three fresh strawberries and a pinch of allspice. Whip this up saying:

"All sickness away, only health may stay.
Where this goes, healing flows!"

Drink to internalize the magick.

♦ ♦ ♦

These activities allow you to become an active participant in your own well-being, but be sure you don't overlook common sense in the process. If you're not getting enough rest, change your life's patterns. If you're not getting better, see a doctor. Witches recognize that medicine is a partner in health. Spells, rituals, meditations, and potions can always be added to this process to fulfill your spiritual thirst.

Magick on the Go

More and more Witches live in urban environments, so we tend to come up with little bits of magick to help us find parking spots, find seats on the bus, protect our cars, or safeguard ourselves when riding the subway. Here are some specific spells along these lines for you to try:

Great Squat

Squat is the goddess of good parking places. When you drive into a crowded parking lot continue reciting the following until you find a parking space:

"GREAT SQUAT, I NEED A SPOT!"

Alternatively, I've found calling on de-"meter" works. Offer her a quarter and you'll get what you want.

Portable Altars

This is a neat all-purpose magickal device for your car. To make one, you'll need an empty container that easily fits in your glove compartment or under your seat. You'll also need some ashes taken from a ritual fire (Fire); a feather or incense (Air); a crystal, soil, or herbs (Earth); and a seashell, kelp, or salt water (Water). Place each of these tokens in your container while saying:

"FIRE AND SEA, SAFETY BE WITH ME.

EARTH AND AIR, FOREVER TAKE CARE!"

Each time you feel you need extra protection in your car, touch the token and repeat the invocation to release the magick. After you've used it four times, I recommend refreshing the components.

You can create a pocket-sized version of this amulet to keep you safe in settings such as a subway or a commuter train.

Lucky Bus Token

Any bus token (or card) will do for this spell, but it's best to use one you're not likely to spend accidentally. (You want to keep it as a charm.) Hold the card or token in your hand. Visualize the bus always coming on time, and visualize a seat for you. Say:

"LET THE BUS BE ON TIME, WITH THE READING OF THIS RHYME.

AND FOR MY COMFORT, LEAVE A SEAT.

BY MY WILL, THIS SPELL'S COMPLETE!"

As you wait for the bus, rub the token in your strong hand and mentally recite the incantation to activate the magick.

As you can see, there's little, if nothing, that cannot be approached with a magickal mindset throughout the day, as long as you're willing to be a little inventive and trust your instincts.

Chapter 9

Magick Through-out the Year

Hours have wings and fly up to the author of time and carry news of our usage

—Milton

After working magick into our daily routines, the next step is following suit throughout the year. There are a few glitches to overcome, however. For example, those of us who live in urban environments find it hard to focus on rituals with barking dogs, ringing phones, or arguing neighbors in the background. Those of us with busy schedules also often find we can't even celebrate a holiday or observance on the right date because of conflicting duties!

Witches realize that working with Nature's cycles is very important for reconnecting to the Earth. When doing so, we find profound symbolism and lessons that are essential to our magickal growth. But in creating an annual calendar for Witches, the other difficulties mentioned here have to be kept in mind.

Thankfully, the world's spiritual traditions provide some answers to this quandary.

Every day, somewhere in the world, there's a festival or celebration happening. This might commemorate a cultural event or a point on the Sacred Wheel, uplift the Divine, or honor a personal or community happening, such as the birth of a child. Whatever the cause for a festival, the sheer number of holidays provides the creative Witch with tremendous flexibility in his or her celebratory schedule. If, for example, you can't celebrate Halloween (Celtic New Year) on its traditional day, you can look for either a New Year's festival or a Festival for the Dead in another culture whose date figures nicely into your schedule. You can then thoughtfully adapt the traditions of that festival into your ritual, and commemorate *both* occasions in the process.

I do not suggest doing this without a little forethought, or without regard for the rich cultural heritage from which a holiday originates. Success really depends on your outlook and the gentility with which you approach the process of research and adaptation. My only caution is being sure you're not including something in your personal reworking that would be abhorrent to the society from which the event comes. For example, don't use pork as part of a post-ritual feast when adapting a Jewish celebration for magick!

With that said, I have combined ancient and modern festivals from around the globe into this chapter, including many that appear on your everyday calendar. Many of these are celebrated around the world; for those celebrations specific to a particular country or region, I've indicated ways that Witches can adapt the tradition. Additionally, I've detailed seasonal overviews with ideas for home and altar decorations, activities, and ways to incorporate your personal magickal tradition into specific celebrations. As you review these, please bear in mind that the exact dates for many holidays shift from year to year, depending on the lunar cycle and other specifications. Check your calendar to confirm the date as you plan your celebration.

I live in a four-season climate; if you don't, you might need to change the activities and suggestions given to better suit your environment. Also, consider adding more personalized celebrations into this rough outline, such as traditions from your heritage, or celebrations that honor what's happening in your life. This way you can continue the rhythm of magick throughout each day of the year in personally meaningful ways.

As the Wheel of Time turns, the seasons come and go, creating an annual rhythm that the ancients studied and followed in their magick. They used the symbolism provided by the Earth and the heavens as a guide for everything from planting and harvesting crops to healing. Following this example, we need to consider each season's symbolic value to our magickal efforts. We also need to look at various adaptable holidays within each season to honor personal, social, or planetary cycles and extend positive energy where it's most needed.

Spring

Spring is the dawning of the resurrected Earth, when trees stretch to meet the sun and everything on the land rejoices with restored vitality. Magickally, this season represents the Maiden or youthful Goddess aspect, whose hopeful vision and energy fill the well of our souls. Spells, rituals, and other magickal methods that focus on inspiration, creativity, and new beginnings are all augmented by timing them for Spring, especially when combined with a waxing moon (first quarter).

Throughout Spring, decorate your altar with fresh-mowed grass, wildflowers, the first buds of a tree, eggs to represent fertility, and seedlings. Spring rain is perfect for the ritual cup or for aspersing the sacred circle. Wear pastel clothing to honor the fresh winds of change and rebirth common to this season, and use your kitchen broom to sweep your home clean of any lingering dark clouds from Winter. Open your windows and doors to welcome the season and good fortune.

Spring Holidays, Festivals, and Observances

Earth Day: late March/early to mid-April

While most Witches will tell you that every day should be Earth Day in the way we treat the planet, this rather new holiday gives everyone a moment to focus our attention on Gaia. Put some physical and metaphysical energy into helping heal the Earth. Plant a tree with loving care or scatter some wildflower seeds into a field with a wish for wholeness.

Smell the Breeze Day (Egypt): March 27

All sects in Egypt observe this holiday with various traditions. An onion was traditionally broken open and smelled for good fortune. Wearing bright colors and going on picnics is the order of the day—the winds improving the health of all. This tradition is very easy to follow. If you're not fond of onions, simply leave one on your altar; if you are, make onion soup and eat it to internalize the lucky nature of this day. If weather doesn't permit taking a walk, just open a window and get a breath of fresh, healthful air instead.

Easter: late March/early April

Easter was named after the ancient Saxon goddess of fertility, Eostre. The symbol of the egg became nearly universal because it represents the Earth's rebirth after Winter. Traditionally the magick circle celebrates this life force today, often with colored eggs and hot cross buns, which represent the solar wheel, for protection. Take time with friends and family to enjoy the warming weather. The sun is now free of Winter's grasp to shine brightly on all your efforts.

April Fool's Day: April 1

On this great holiday for the child within all of us, work magick that will improve your sense of humor today. Tickle your aura happy with a feather. I'd also suggest that this might be the perfect time to contemplate the wisdom of fools by meditating on the Fool Card of the tarot.

National Folk Festival: second weekend in April

This festival is held annually in St. Louis, Missouri, complete with all manner of folk arts and crafts, from sword dancing to bell ringing and lumber jack competitions. For me, this is a time to go digging through books of folklore and superstition to find the nuggets of magickal gold housed therein. For hundreds of years this is where witchy wisdom was hidden—and it's still there waiting for us to rediscover and apply in our everyday world.

May Day/Beltane: May 1

This holiday originates with the Romans, who looked for any good excuse for a party. It's traditional to gather blossoming flowers today and give them anonymously to a kind-hearted person, dance the May pole for fertility (figurative or literal), fire leap for luck, wash in May dew for beauty, purify yourself or your pets by passing through the smoke of a ritual fire, and meditate on the power of masculine-feminine energies combining.

Ceremony for Rain (Guatemala): May 11

This ritual is overseen by local priests who pray to the gods and goddesses for aid, beginning in the village center then all around town at each shrine. After five days, the ritual culminates in a community dance complete with rain sticks and maracas that create the sound of rain as a kind of sympathetic magick. For today's Witches this might translate into a day to direct weather magick toward areas of the planet where it's most needed. Alternatively, perform rituals and spells to turn away emotional storms that might be headed your way.

Feast of Isidro (Philippines): May 15

Isidro, the patron saint of the harvest in this part of the world, trusted in angels to aid needy farmers. After the rice is gathered, the streets of Manila fill with people carrying yams, flowers, coconut, sugarcane, and nature fruits, all of which are displayed lavishly. For us, this might be a good opportunity to bless our seeds and soil before planting. If you wish, call on Isidro to empower your efforts. Alternatively, consider the metaphoric value in this holiday: What attributes do you wish to cultivate and harvest later in the year (think faith, peace, joy, and so forth)? Work magick toward those ends.

Well Dressing (Britain): any May Sunday

Throughout Britain there are wells dedicated to the saints and various powerful in-dwelling spirits. During the month of May, these wells receive offerings of flowers or coins to inspire healing, guidance, prosperity, or an answer to other wishes. To adapt this, focus on Water-related magick or wishcraft today.

Night of Observation: early June

This is the beginning of Ramadan, a time of fasting in Moslem lands that commemorates Adam's exile from Eden. For Witches, this could be a time for introspection and pondering the dark side of the soul. Fasting is perfectly apt, as it cleanses the body and hones the spirit.

Night of the Drop (Egypt): June 16

Once a year the Nile drops to reveal the rich soil that sustains the region's entire economy. This is a joyous celebration filled with divinatory efforts and sacred readings. Following suit, you might want to try some new divination tools today, or read over your Book of Shadows looking for new insights.

Summer

Summer is the season during which the fire of vitality flows through the land. The sun prances high in the sky, and everything beneath is lively and active. This is also the season for following magick with tangible efforts, and for spells focused on dramatic transformation, power, and socialization. Study your Craft under a shady tree where the Mother/Father aspect of the Divine can speak directly to your heart, filling it with the light of insight.

Place a few extra candles and a fire agate on your altar to celebrate the Fire Element, and add reds or oranges to the sacred space. By all means, don't forget to use your candles in divination (pyromancy)! If you have a place for bonfires, make one and dance around it, adding some aromatic fire herbs, such as cinnamon, to the kindling.

Summer Holidays, Festivals, and Observances

Midsummer's Day/Summer Solstice: June 21

This festival of fire and water was likely first celebrated by the Romans. Generally fires are lit today, and wreaths are tossed into the ritual flames along with the participants' wishes. You can then carry the ashes with you as a charm for abundance or scatter them in your garden to improve its yield. Decorate your altar with traditional touches, such as birch, fennel, and lily, and watch out for fairy folk who might take up residence in a nearby rose bush! Consider casting spells that focus on mental clarity or physical strength.

Day of the Seven Sleepers: June 27

An old Muslim story tells us that six people went into a cave to test their faith in God. A dog guarded the cave's entrance, and the people fell asleep inside and remained there for more than 300 years. For his devotion, the dog is now in paradise overseeing matters of communication.

Because of this tale, Muslims never say they'll do something tomorrow unless it's followed by the phrase "if God pleases!"

I think this is a good example to follow. If you're a procrastinator, cast spells for motivation today. Carry a statue of a dog to remind you to stay focused.

Independence Day (United States): July 4

While the nation celebrates its freedom from England, this is a good time for Witches to celebrate religious freedom and pray that it continues. It's also an effective time to cast spells or work rituals that will help liberate you from anything that binds and holds you back.

Panathenaea (Greece): July 10

This five-day festival honored Athena, the goddess of wisdom. Races, regattas, and musical exhibitions were followed on the sixth day by an offering of a new robe to the goddess. This, along with fruit, grain, and bread was thought to ensure her blessings. If Athena is your patroness, definitely take time to honor her today. For others, this might be a good day to look for a new ritual robe or work magick directed toward personal wisdom.

Binding of the Wreaths (Lithuania): July 20

On this day young lovers go to the forest gathering flowers for wreaths, under which they kiss. Once this is done the couple "dates" for at least a year. For modern Witches this is a suitable alternative to May Day festivities and for timing any type of love and commitment magick. Notably, July is the traditional Roman month for marriage. If you choose to wed on this day, have some flower wreaths or birch branch decorations to connect you to the positive energy of this lovely ancient rite.

Lammas: August 1

One of the four major Druidic festivals, Lammas is a celebration of early harvested food. Literally, Lammas means "loaf mass," and it is still traditional to bake bread today for ongoing providence. If you're not a great cook (or are pressed for time), buy frozen bread dough and knead in some herbs that represent maintaining good health, such as a teaspoon of rosemary, or other pressing needs in your life. Give a little of this bread to the birds before you partake. They will carry your wishes across the land.

Festival of the Minstrel: August 16

This holiday dates back to 13th-century Medieval Europe, when Bardic tradition was very important to maintaining histories. On this day, elaborate feasts, stories, and songs filled the land, and one artisan was chosen above the rest for his or her talents. Following suit, you might want to practice your own talents today and ask for blessings upon them. Additionally, pray for the ongoing creativity of the New Age/magickal artists who fill our lives with beauty and inspiration.

Festival of the Green Corn: August 25

This lovely festival, celebrated in New York state, honors Native Americans, their lore, and their traditions. If you're a Witch with strong shamanic leanings, today's the perfect time to study further. Meditate on the world tree and its meaning in your life. Go to a natural setting and get closer to the land, as our native ancestors tried to teach us.

Festival of Durga (Bengal): September 7

Durga is the Hindu goddess of Earth and power, and the wise wife of Shiva. This date marks the start of a five-day celebration in her honor, dedicated mostly to family reunions and burying any old "axes" one bears against family members. This can have tremendous merit in a magickal setting as a forgiveness ritual, where we try and make amends with those from whom we've been estranged. Even if you can't get together with those people, cast a welcoming spell in their direction to open the path for healing to begin.

Birthday of the Moon (China): September 15

This is a perfect day that can substitute for any missed lunar ritual. In Chinese tradition, the moon represents the Goddess, and this is her birthday. On this day it's customary to bathe in moon-light and eat moon-shaped cakes to connect with the universe's powerful Yin energies. We can follow suit, adding spells for in-sight, fertility, and any other lunar-related magickal themes.

Fall

Fall sits with quiet grace between Summer and Winter, life and death. It is a season suited to magick that focuses on endings, facing personal shadows, emotional healing, reaping the rewards of honest labors, prudence, and careful consideration of one's goals. Potential decorations for your altar and sacred space include a moonstone, pearly hues, fall leaves, late-blooming flow-ers, braided corn husks, and harvest foods. Don robes of a darker hue, and fill the ritual cup with apple cider, a traditional Fall favorite.

Fall Holidays, Festivals, and Observances

Birthday of the Sun/Autumn Equinox: September 21

Among Peruvians, the Autumn Equinox is a time of cleans-ing and putting one's house in order. It's customary to greet the sun at dawn with invocations and music and to present an offer-ing of wine to the Earth. For magickal folk, we, too, focus on balance and order, bearing in mind that the sun will soon begin to wane. This holiday also marks the second harvest, for which we should give thanks and carefully store for Winter.

Divali (India): September 26

This is the start of a new business year, which oddly coin-cides with the Feast of Lamps honoring the dead. Not surpris-ingly, the holiday focuses on Lakshmi, the goddess of prosperity. Tradition dictates that moving into a new home bodes well today, that you should pay all bills and wash your money with milk to safeguard your wealth, and that putting a blessed coin in your checkbook will bring money your way. All of these activities work very well in a magickal setting, especially if they are augmented with green or gold candles and suitable incantations for improved finances, business sense, better jobs, and the like.

New Year's (Morocco): October 3

This celebration is filled with magickal properties that we can borrow. Burning straw on the rooftop will protect you from evil today, and the resulting ashes are an excellent amulet against disease. Wash in the morning for health, and sprinkle water around the sacred space of home to protect all who dwell therein. Decorate your altar with pennyroyal, thyme, and rosemary for safety (not to mention that these herbs deter flies). And, as part of your ritual, dab yourself with rosewater for physical beauty.

Floating of the Lamps (Siam): October 13

This festival of lights honors the Buddha. Small rafts are decorated with flowers and put out to float on the river so Buddha can see and be pleased by them. Monks often begin a period of retreat after this date, so they're presented with various gifts to help meet their needs, such as money or clothing. This last part gives me pause to consider how many of our magickal leaders we've truly supported in word and deed. If there's a way you can give something back to them or your magickal community, do so today!

Kuan Yin Day (China): mid-October

Kuan Yin is the goddess who protects wives and children; this feast celebrates the anniversary of her death. At this time of year, people leave offerings at her shrines throughout China to receive beauty, compassion, and protection. Young women will often receive the gift of a goddess statue today, which represents a happy, harmonious home. In keeping with the symbolism here, whatever your choice of goddess, light a candle and invoke her blessings today. Specifically, ask for the safety and well-being of the women and children who bless your life.

Samhain (Halloween): October 31

Tonight, spirits and fairy folk freely visit the Earth. The Celts celebrated New Year's by taking care of legal matters, making peace within communities, and honoring their ancestors. In magickal circles even today, these traditions hold true. The past and future, spirit and temporal, meet together in the sacred space, encouraging effective divinatory efforts. By all means put a carved pumpkin or turnip on your altar—these were made to protect against unwanted spiritual guests!

Feast of Dionysus (Greece): November 11

This was a harvest festival in which new wine was opened and tasted in honor of the god of good cheer. For today's Witch this is a good opportunity to make or bless ritual wines for specific purposes, bearing in mind that in Greek tradition the god and the wine were one and the same! Mead, in particular, is a customary beverage to sip today for good health—just remember to pour out a small libation in thanks to Earth for her fruits.

Thanksgiving: last Thursday in November

I strongly advocate all Witches honoring this American custom, started by the pilgrims at Plymouth Rock, of giving thanks today. Remember, the grateful heart is ready to give and receive. Leave a small bit of your Thanksgiving feast on your altar for your household god/dess and perhaps put some nuts outside for hungry squirrels to bless the Earth and its inhabitants as you've been blessed.

Stray Sale: first Monday in December

Any cattle and horses that somehow wandered into the wrong stable are taken into town squares in Texas to be traded and sold. For Witches this equates to working magick to find lost items.

Hopi Winter Ceremony: December 13

Eight days before the Winter Solstice, the Hopi bid farewell to Fall and welcome Winter in ritual. Special prayer feathers are made to bless the home, each of which represents the wish for a gentle voice, and each person receives a sprouting plant to ensure life, health, and joy. To adapt this a bit, consider smudging your home using a feather to disperse the incense, and plant some seedlings that will keep the sacred space of home green throughout the Winter. Leave these on your altar to symbolize hope to offset the Winter blues.

Winter

Winter is the time of the dark moon, a fallow period when the Earth rests, sound asleep beneath sheets of snow. Yet life still stirs subtly, being nurtured by the silence. During this season, cover your altar with pine needles, pine cones, an acorn (for the hope of Spring), holly, ivy, and other traditional Winter fare. Focus your attention on magick for improving your psychic self and health. For the workaholics out there, let Winter teach you the valuable lesson of rest.

Winter Holidays, Festivals, and Observances

December Moon (Alaska): full moon

For modern Witches this equates to an alternative Earth Day celebration in which we might want to abstain from meat. The Eskimos believe that animals have souls, and on this day the spirits of creatures who provide food and other substances are appeased with hymns and prayers as part of a special celebration of gratitude.

Winter Solstice/Yule: December 21

The ancient Druids picked mistletoe today, while Europeans brought evergreen boughs into their homes to appease the Nature spirits. Holly and ivy protected homes from wandering spirits, and candles chased away the night and supported the sun's struggle to overcome the darkness. For Witches, this has become a time to celebrate with family and friends, reveling in our common bonds. It's also a date to honor one's heritage and traditions with a flurry of panache. Consider working spells for luck, health, and prosperity today, all of which will benefit from this timing.

New Year's Day: January 1

Yet another alternative to Hallows, we neatly usher out the old year today and welcome a new beginning. Open your windows to open the way for new perspective. Sweep out any lingering depression with a broom, take out a divination tool for perspective on the coming months, and leave an offering on your altar as a way of thanking the Divine for last year's blessings.

Justica's Day (Rome): January 8

This goddess of fairness, considered to be very ethical and sensible, was worshiped in Rome on this day. Today's Witch could do well to also remember this goddess today, considering how much sensibility we need in handling both our spiritual and mundane lives effectively. Also call upon her if you have pending legal matters that need rectification.

Festival of Sarasvati (Asia): mid- to late January

The goddess of wisdom and learning is highly sought after today. Honor her with gifts of incense and white flowers. Students in particular should bring books, pens, and other symbols of education to statues of the goddess for her blessing. Following in this custom, modern Witches might want to eat "brain" foods, such as walnuts and fish, today and enact various rituals/spells to improve the conscious mind. Burn rosemary incense to augment this goal vibrationally, because rosemary is a memory herb.

New Year of the Trees (Palestine): January 23

A lovely Earth Day-styled celebration, this festival needs no tweaking to be magickal as it stands. It's customary today to plant trees, one each for an honored loved one who has recently passed over. If you cannot plant a tree, take a moment to remember the people in your life who have blessed you, and pray for their peace. Honor their memory with stories and photos, and perhaps celebrate a special ritual that sends positive energy toward renewing the Earth as they do in Palestine.

Feast of the Kitchen God (China): late January

The Kitchen God is the guardian of moral virtue in Chinese homes. Each year in late January this protector reports to the Pearly Emperor in heaven on the family's behavior. Before he leaves, the family sends him off with offerings of cakes and candies (so his words will be sweet).

In my home I like to give the Kitchen God the day off and go out for food instead. Alternatively, make a lavish feast to celebrate your culinary skills and the positive influence of your hearth god or goddess has had on kitchen magick of any sort.

Candlemas/Bridge's Day/Groundhog Day: February 1 and 2

This ancient festival, with strong roots in Germanic and Irish tradition, marks the first hopeful signs of Spring returning to the Earth. This is an excellent day to perform spells and rituals for luck, health, prosperity, or the well-being of animals. Adorn your altar with white candles to give strength to the sun.

Chinese New Year: February

The first day of February's full moon ignites this Fire festival with potent protective energy. Traditionally, noisemakers and light sources chased away any evil influences in people's lives. Today it is a time to honor ancestors and can act as an alternative festival for the dead.

In China, people leave offerings for departed ancestors at their graves or at a shrine at home, focus on family unity, and follow various folk traditions to inspire longevity and good fortune (especially with money). There is no reason for you not to follow suit, decorating your altar with oranges, burning juniper incense, and eating the ritual meal with chopsticks.

Mass for the Broken Needles: February 8

The art of the seamstress is highly valued in Japan, and this is a day for honoring all the broken and bent needles as part of that art. Magickally speaking, this translates into honoring the tools of your art, be they magickal or mundane, and blessing them for continued use.

Valentine's Day: February 14

This event grew out of an old Roman tradition where young people would draw lots to discover their soon-to-be lover. And even among today's pragmatic Witches, it's a perfect occasion to cast spells and try divinations that focus on matters of love and romance. Renew your marriage vows; tell loved ones how much you appreciate them. If your patron goddess is Venus or Aphrodite (or a similar god/dess) you might want to honor her on your altar to encourage lasting affection in your home.

President's Day: third Monday in February

First observed in the late 1700s, this holiday represents a great opportunity for Witches everywhere to send out positive energy to our Wiccan and world leaders, specifically for the wisdom and insight to create a peaceful future for all humankind.

Terminalia (Rome): February 23

Once a year the Romans went around their personal land, marking the borders with garlands and offerings to the god Terminus, who oversees perimeters. This kept the land safe and fertile for another year. Translating this into modern Witchery isn't difficult. Simply use this timing for spells and rituals focused on protecting and supporting the sacred space of home. If you do have a garden, this is also a great date for blessing the soil, magickally preparing it for your witchy herbs or edibles.

New Year: March 10

As this event unfolds, people in Siam wear rings of unspun cord over their shoulders for protection, bless their animals, and go to temple to honor their faith. If you'd like to adapt this as an alternative New Year's or blessing rite, simply find some yarn and unravel it. White is a good color choice because it represents protection. Place this in areas needing safety. Take a moment to pray for your pets, and light a candle at your altar to welcome the Sacred into your life.

A Personal Book of Days

As you go through the year, keep notes about the holidays and celebrations that you've tried and/or adapted. Make sure to include what personally significant changes you made, and whether or not you felt the results were successful. You can return to this information year after year for insights and ideas. With time, you'll begin building a Book of Days that celebrates and commemorates the seasons, personal occasions, and magick in very meaningful ways. Keep this collection safe. It can and will become part of your family's heritage, something to pass on so that Witches of future generations have a prototype upon which to build their vision of the Craft.

Afterword

Witches today know that our "job" isn't limited to specific hours or days. Magick is something we live and become; it can't be sequestered from the rest of our reality if it's to have meaning and power.

In the future, I suspect our lives are going to be no less hectic or complex. Use rituals and other magickal events as a way to add richness to everyday life and to honor your magickal path. Don't let the metaphysical potential in any moment pass you by so that your Witchery always grows and changes with you, the Earth, and the Universe.

The best part about modern Witchcraft is that our adventure is really just beginning. We have a potent recipe for building a tomorrow where magick will shine without fear or apology.

To the future!

Appendix

Note: Some of the older books on this list are out of print. They are still available at libraries.

Amulets & Superstitions
E.A. Wallis Budge
Oxford University Press, 1930

Beyond the Blue Horizon
Dr. E.C. Krupp
Oxford University Press, 1992

Book of Plant Uses, Names, and Folklore
Ron Freethy
Tanager Books, 1985

Crystal, Gem & Metal Magic
Scott Cunningham
Llewellyn Publications, 1995

Culpeper's Herbal
D. Potterton, editor
Sterling Publishing, 1983

Curious Lore of Precious Stones
George Frederick Kunz
Dover Publications, 1971

The Dictionary of Omens & Superstitions
Philippa Waring
Chartwell Books, 1978

A Dictionary of Superstitions
Iona Opie and Moira Tatem
Oxford University Press, 1989

Encyclopedia of Magical Herbs
Scott Cunningham
Llewellyn Publications, 1988

Encyclopedia of Myths and Legends
Stuart Gordon
Headline Book Publishing, 1993

The Encyclopedia of the Occult
Lewis Spence
Bracken Books, 1988

Everyday Life Through the Ages
Michael Worth Davison, editor
Reader's Digest Association Ltd.,
1992

Everyday's a Holiday
Ruth Hutchinson
Harper and Brothers, 1961

Futuretelling
Patricia Telesco
Crossing Press, 1997

Global Ritualism
Denny Sargent
Llewellyn Publications, 1994

Goddesses in World Mythology
Martha Ann & Dorothy Myers
Imel
Oxford University Press, 1995

Green Magic
Leslie Gordon
Viking Press, 1977

Herbal Arts
Patricia Telesco
Citadel Press, 1997

Herbal Magick
Paul Beyerl
Phoenix Publishing, 1998

A History of Magic
Richard Cavendish
Taplinger Publishing, 1979

Illustrated Book of Signs & Symbols
Miranda Bruce-Mitford
DK Publishing, 1996

Kitchen Witch's Cookbook
Patricia Telesco
Llewellyn Publications, 1994

The Language of Dreams
Patricia Telesco
Crossing Press, 1997

Magic in Food
Scott Cunningham
Llewellyn Publications, 1991

*New Larousse Encyclopedia of
Mythology*
Richard Aldington, translator
Hamlyn Publishing, 1973

Oracles and Divination
Michael Loewe and Carmen
Blacker, editors
Shambhala, 1981

Perfumery & Kindred Arts
R.S. Cristiani
Baird and Company: 1877

Please Understand Me
David Keirsey
Prometheus Books, 1978

Rodale's Illustrated Encyclopedia of Herbs
Claire Kowalchik and William Hylton, editors
Rodale Press, 1987

Secret Teachings of All Ages
Manley P. Hall
Philosophical Research Society, 1977

Spells and How They Work
Jane and Stewart Farrar
Phoenix, 1990

Standard Dictionary of Folklore, Mythology, and Legend
Maria Leach, editor
Harper & Row, 1984

Ten Thousand Dreams Interpreted
Gastavus Hindman Miller
M.A. Donohuse & Co., 1931

Totems
Brad Steiger
HarperCollins, 1996

Witch's Brew
Llewellyn Publications, 1995

The Woman's Dictionary of Symbols & Sacred Objects
Barbara Walker
Harper & Row, 1988

Index

About the Author

Trish Telesco has more than 30 books on the market, including *Goddess in My Pocket*, *The Herbal Arts*, and *Kitchen Witch's Cookbook*, each of which represents a different area of spiritual interest. While her actual Wiccan education was originally self-trained and self-initiated, Trish later received initiation into the Strega tradition of Italy, which gives form and fullness to the folk magick she practices.

Trish travels the country lecturing and offering book signings. She has appeared on several television segments, including one for *Sightings* on multicultural divination systems and one for the *Debra Duncan Show* on modern Wicca. In addition, Trish writes for metaphysical journals and mainstream publications, including *Circle Network News*, *Magical Blend*, *Complete Woman*, and *Woman's World*. Readers can visit Trish's home page at *www.loresinger.com* or her Yahoo club at *www.clubs.yahoo.com/clubs/folkmagicwithtrishtelesco*.

She lives in western New York with her husband, three children, and several pets.